HARVEY HAVOC

THE FUTURE IS HAVOC

BY

AVERY A. BELL

2019

LAUGHING SKULL MEDIA

―――――――

Text by Avery A. Bell

Graphics by Clare Bohning

2019

ISBN: 978-0-578-53119-9

Edited by Lara Milton of Spectrum Editing

Consultant: Kirsten Anthony—drugs expert, fellow crime connoisseur, and oldest friend from low places.

―――――――

Averybellsgarage.com

DEDICATION

For all the misfits. May you find your island and reign.

CHAPTER 1

DISMAL NIGHT

"Shit, why the hell didn't I aim for his head instead of his shoulder?"

I reach the top of the sprawling concrete staircase as the words escape my lips. My lungs pump in the dank air, and I step onto the landing in front of me.

"Three damn city blocks and a dozen flights of stairs? Harvey, what the hell were you thinking?"

I can't answer my own question. Outside this abandoned apartment building, the dark streets of Motor City are punctuated with the sick glow emanating from her LED street signs. Her once-decaying structures have been reanimated by haphazard progress. In a strange way, it feels as if the city wants me to kill the man I've been chasing.

You'd be doing the whole city a favor, Harvey. There are too many people in this world already.

"No."

I take in a deep breath and then exhale. "I can't do that. I *won't* do that."

Calling myself out doesn't take the edge off, but knowing that the chance of civilian casualties decreased as soon as we entered this building is enough to push me forward. I use the training the police academy drilled into my head to determine how best to proceed down the dark hallway ahead of me. At just over six feet tall, I instinctively duck to avoid colliding with a hanging ceiling tile.

It's more than probable that only one of us will walk out of this building alive. I've also managed to stack the deck against myself by leaving my bulletproof vest in the car. I'm facing a possible gunfight in a leather jacket and jeans; perfect.

You should have killed Johnathan. That would have been so much easier.

"Shut up."

To my left is the first door in the hall. It's closed. I try to focus and calm myself to detect any possible sound. After a moment, I hear rapid breathing resonating from within the room. I wonder if he's just winded or if I actually hit him when I aimed for his shoulder earlier. I risk a tap of the small fingerprint-sensitive button on the edge of my transponder's screen, and the word "Received" passes across its three-by-five transparent face. I place it safely back in my inner jacket pocket. Reinforcements will be here soon.

I move lightly on my feet and turn my back to the wall next to the doorframe. I choose to shorten his name; it's a feeble tactic to try to gain his trust. "John, this doesn't have to end badly."

At first there's no reply, though I can still hear heavy breathing.

"I know you're in there. I just want the chance to talk," I say.

"Why ... bother?" Johnathan asks, his voice faint, with a long pause between the words.

"Because I don't want to kill you."

"You must've pushed ... the call button ... already. How long ... have I got?"

I consider telling him that no one knows we're here, but I doubt a former officer would believe such an obvious lie. "Maybe a few minutes. Probably less."

"Shit. SHIT!" Johnathan yells, his words labored by his exhaustion.

"Look, I know you served. We both know what's coming next. I'm only doing my job."

"Yeah? I did my ... fucking job too. All three years of ... goddamned mandatory service." Johnathan's voice has taken on an air of desperation. We both fall silent for a time, catching our breath.

"I was at the crime scene earlier today," I say after a while. "It looked like an accident to me."

"So what? It doesn't matter, does it? You know I killed my wife, accident or not."

"Come on, man," I urge him. "Just come out quietly and we can end this mess. You can forget this whole thing and start a different life. You won't even remember today."

Johnathan isn't falling for it. "I know how it fucking works. Either you kill me or you erase my memory and turn me into a fucking vegetable."

Instinctively, I rest my hand on my gun. There's no use in arguing against the truth. "You better make up your mind quick.

When the other officers get here, they're only going to be looking to make quota." The words taste as bitter as the corruption they represent.

"You're Harvey, right?" Johnathan asks, his voice now strangely calm.

"Yeah, Harvey Havoc."

"Well, Harvey, I didn't mean to hurt my wife. It was just a stupid fight. I pushed her, and she tripped over the arm of the sofa. As soon as her head hit the cabinet, I knew."

"I understand. If it really happened as you say, then you have nothing to run from. Let me help you out of this."

The sound of sirens drowns out his reply as the squad cars begin to pull up outside. The time for a quiet conversation is at a close; the opportunity to end this pleasantly is fading.

"John, you need to come out of there. We're running out of time."

"Thank you, Harvey."

"For what?"

"For believing me about my wife."

"I was just looking at the evidence."

"You're a rare one, then. All the same, I have no plans of letting them take my mind from me. I can do that myself."

The shot reverberates through the wall behind me, desolation cutting through me as the bullet rips through Johnathan. The sound of a stampede of boots echoes up the staircase from the hall behind me. I give the door a firm kick, and the rotten wood splinters around the ancient lock. I find Johnathan's body slumped on the floor inside the entryway.

The long-abandoned apartment he chose to die in is lit only by a broken-out window at the far end of the room.

The fetid smell from the hall is more extreme within. The water-saturated walls are stained with rust and mold. I see that my shot from before tore a large chunk of flesh from Johnathan's left shoulder. His devastatingly placed bullet entered from under his jaw, and despite the poor light, I can see the dark residue of the powder burn left in its wake. The blood oozing from the entry wound is nothing compared to the much-larger exit wound; a pattern composed of blood and brains has erupted backward onto the wall. I bend down and press my fingers onto Johnathan's carotid artery. It's more force of habit than anything else. His pale skin already feels cool to the touch.

In the Motor City Police Department, there are three generally accepted ends to the pursuit of a suspect. The first is a clean, single-shot kill. It's by far the department's most preferred method, though they would never say that outright. The second is a nonviolent takedown. It results in more paperwork, but is considered the humane option. Those who are arrested and found guilty have their minds erased at a purpose-built facility over a six-month period, if their crime is heinous enough. They are then chemically sterilized before being assigned work in the manufacturing industry. It's all part of the plan for the greater good of our teeming population. Johnathan took the third option. He chose his own way out. *In this ever-darkening age,* I think, *death was the best thing for him.*

The two officers who show up first in the hall outside are Metzler and Harris. They hold the record for meeting quota in our department.

"Fuck, looks like Pretty Boy Havoc got the kill," Metzler says as his lungs, burdened by his girth, labor to recover from the climb. His slick voice and cheap suit make the blood begin to boil in my veins. I turn to face him. Metzler is one of those self-centered angry types, his ego twice his considerable size. An insidious beetle of a man.

"Well, isn't that just great? Biggest payday any of us could've had in a fucking month, and you let the shithead off himself?" Harris is almost frothing at the mouth. Just shy of my height, Harris is a thin man, his loose-fitting khakis paired poorly with an oversized polo shirt. He has a bulletproof vest on underneath it, probably less for protection than to make his lanky frame appear larger than it actually is. His eyes are narrow. His bristly black mustache is almost overshadowed by the width of his nostrils.

"For fuck's sake, he used to be your partner!" I yell.

"So what?" asks Metzler.

"So show some fucking respect, for a start."

Neither of them appreciates my reply. Harris's wide nostrils flare even wider, and Metzler squares his shoulders. I take the high road and brush past both of them. I don't acknowledge the other officers I pass as I make my way toward the staircase. There's no reason to blame them for how this night went. Anyway, it's all my fault. I should've taken the chance and broken down the door. Talking gave Johnathan the time to work up enough determination to kill himself. More important than my feelings is the fact that I don't have the patience for a pissing contest right now. A fight with Metzler and Harris would be a complete waste of my time. I head down the stairs quickly, trying to put as much distance as I can between myself and the experience I've just endured.

Once I'm outside, I take a series of deep breaths in an attempt to compose myself. The air on the street isn't as musty as inside, but the iron in it tastes of blood mixed with a hint of burn-barrel smoke and the bitter sweetness of antifreeze. The wind picks up. Its chill makes my tired muscles ache. An officer is dead, and I could do nothing to stop it.

Metzler and Harris are the scum of the department; however, in this instance, they also have the frustrating distinction of being partially correct. With Johnathan's suicide, there will be no one getting paid tonight. Hours of difficult pursuit put to an unexpected and dismal end for all parties involved. If I could've talked him down, I would've made something of the evening. I could've used the extra money. It's been almost a month since my last successful pursuit.

Told you, says the city.

I rub my eyes and ignore her.

There's a fine line between success and failure as an officer in the Serenity Division of the MCPD. If you don't have any takedowns in a given month, you're considered inept. Too many, and you look bloodthirsty. Protests and marches have been held over that last part, and none of them have been unfounded.

But if you're facing mandatory service, your choices get narrowed down pretty quickly. Landing somewhere in the middle is safest.

Metzler and Harris are on the far end of the spectrum, taking their quota right up to the unspoken highest acceptable rate of five kills in a month. I hover right above the bottom line. The bounty I make is usually enough to scrape by financially and maintain a small amount of self-respect. At least the MCPD provides a free transponder and medical benefits second to none; otherwise, there would be little reprieve for anyone in service.

I wait just beyond the crowd of officers, resolved not to leave until I see them take Johnathan's body out. I'm hoping it will bring me some kind of closure. After a while, the coroner brings out the stretcher holding his neatly bagged corpse. This doesn't calm my nerves as I had hoped. It does provide a reason for me to return to the station, though I'd rather not give my report tonight.

I begin to walk the three blocks to my car. As I progress, I see things more clearly than before. The buildings I dismissively ran past earlier loom over me menacingly. The holes in the sidewalk have a greater potential of tripping me up. People on the street become more of a threat as my senses acclimate to this particular Motor City nightscape.

I pass by an old vagrant huddled in the corner where two immense brick buildings meet, his resting place no doubt chosen for its proximity to a nearby sewage grate, the steam rising from it providing a source of heat and an overpowering odor. I pause as I realize Johnathan and I must've run past the old man less than an hour ago. To him, our struggle was not as important as his rest. I stand there longer than I would like to admit, envying him for choosing his method of survival instead of mine. Eventually, I turn my attention away from him to proceed the remaining distance to my car.

My path is blocked by a middle-aged businessman with a fine suit and well-groomed hair. He stands out in this neighborhood like oil in water. The late hour amplifies the unusualness of his presence here. His back is turned to me as I approach. When I draw near, he turns toward me.

"What an odd vehicle to see."

I assume his words are directed at me, but he's looking past me. Unsettled by the blank expression on his pale face, I rest my hand on my gun before replying. "Yeah, she's different, for sure."

"I used to be in politics before I was in business, you know. Now I work for the company I helped create," he says vaguely.

"Really?"

"I helped write the laws back in 2050 to prohibit the mass production of new vehicles. That's how Markot Industries got a foothold in the refurbishing business. Old cars given new life is the reason this city got back on its feet again." He looks around at the neon-illuminated smog as if it's something wondrous. "When you think about it like that, people like me made it possible for cars like this to be on the road still." He points toward my hulking white vehicle.

"Maybe I should thank you, then," I say neutrally. "I've saved a bunch of money over the years driving this old girl."

"Yours?" he asks, an eyebrow raised.

I nod. His placid face lights up. I keep my eyes trained on him, but my peripheral vision is on high alert.

"What is it?" he asks.

"1965 Cadillac Superior Crown hearse, 429 V8 under the hood. Her name's Elli. I've done quite a few modifications to her myself over the time I've owned her."

"Amazing. Why a hearse? If you don't mind my asking?"

I shrug. "It unnerves most people. Intimidation tends to keep me alive in my line of work."

"What line of work are you in?"

"I'm an officer in the Serenity Division."

"Ah! We're both in work that society dislikes. None are hated more than politicians, businessmen, and Serenity cops," he chuckles.

His conversation with me is causing serious concern. Abundant friendliness toward strangers is one of the first signs that someone is taking Tech. A volatile synthesis of several of the most dangerous drugs on the street, Tech can have strange effects on a person's mind and their DNA with long-term use. It's no surprise that Tech takes more lives in Motor City than any other cause. I decide to put my hypothesis to the test with a more specific question.

"What brings you to this part of town so late, if you don't mind my asking?" Mimicking his speech pattern may help trigger a slipup, providing proof of my theory.

"Oh, nothing out of the ordinary. Just here to buy some Tech," he says.

Honesty, especially at the user's expense, is another common side effect of the drug. There's a chance for me to salvage this night. Bringing in a Techie will get me some compensation. In fact, it could be beneficial for both of us. After a few months in rehab, if he has committed no major crimes, this guy could even return to normal society.

I pretend his words haven't alarmed me. "What's your name?"

"I'm Ray Adams," he replies. He presents his hand to me. I shake it firmly to avoid suspicion.

"Harvey Havoc."

The color drains from his face. His free hand clenches into a fist and flies toward me. I dodge to the side and narrowly miss getting a broken nose. He draws his fist back and comes at me again. I duck and send a sweeping kick toward his ankles. The blow catches him off guard, toppling him to the ground. He puts out his arms to try to catch himself, but his head glances off the sidewalk. It doesn't knock him out, but it does stun him enough to give me time to restrain him properly. I force him over onto his stomach and cuff his hands behind his back. As I pull him to his feet, he mutters under his breath, "Kill Harvey Havoc."

Closer to his face than I've been before, I recognize him from earlier in the evening. When I pulled into this spot, I saw Johnathan run into Adams as he brushed past. If Johnathan knew Adams was a Techie, he could've planted the thought of killing me in Adams's mind. Had Adams noticed the bar code and name tattoo on the left side of my head as I ran past earlier, he would've attacked me then. Instead, by a twist of fate and poor observation on Adams's part, Johnathan's trap lay in wait for me until now. As I put Adams in the back of the hearse, I perceive Johnathan's darker motives. If he could send an impressionable Techie to kill me, maybe his wife's death wasn't quite the accident it had appeared to be.

As I open my door, the vagrant staggers up. His tattered coat is open just enough to make out the word "Recycled" on the shirt beneath it, with an arrow pointing upward. The noise from my struggle with Adams must've interrupted his slumber.

"Damn copsh," he drunkenly drawls. "Alwaysh tryin' to make their quota. You gonna take me in ash well? Or are you done for the month?"

"I'm just doing my job."

"Whatever you hafta tell yourshelf to shleep at night," he slurs.

The old man stumbles back to his spot as I climb into the huge hearse. She cranks over stubbornly at first, as if to protest that I have loaded her with a dangerous cargo. I am provided with a constant reminder of the evening's events as I drive back to the station. From behind the hearse's divider glass, I hear Adams saying "Kill Harvey Havoc" in an endless loop.

Surprised to find an empty space out front, I park Elli and remove Adams from the back. The Tech is beginning to wear off, and he's lethargic and confused. I have to half push, half pull him all the way to Booking. Since the unofficial motto of the modern department is "Shoot first and ask questions later," Booking is in the most antiquated part of the building. In contrast to the polished marble floors and vaulted ceilings of the main entryway we passed through, its corridors and cells have not been updated in decades. It's as sparsely populated with warm bodies as the average morgue. To my dismay, I realize Carl is on duty tonight. I think he enjoys gossip even more than he enjoys overpressing his uniform.

"Decided to trade in a big fish for a little Techie, huh? If you keep this up, there'll be havoc on the streets soon," he chuckles.

I try to ignore Carl's teasing and bad pun. They only add to my rising temper. If I let him get to me, I'd probably end up punching him in the face, all of my frustration released in one career-ending lapse of judgment. I can't afford that. If he knows of my failure this evening, so does the rest of the department. He takes down the information and then drags Adams back to a holding cell. By morning, he will be mostly himself again. If I get the chance, I could drop back by and ask him who planted the "Kill Harvey Havoc" idea in his head. He might remember, might not. Either way, he will be checked for any prior offenses. If his record is fairly clean, rehab at a state-sanctioned facility will come after that.

All in all, Ray Adams may come out of this evening the least damaged of any of us. This thought gives me some satisfaction as I leave Booking and head for my own division. More updated than Booking, the Serenity wing has been modernized within the decade. It takes up much of the original footprint of the department. Other buildings were added onto it to contain the rest of the vast police force. The largest and lowest division is Street, taking care of the unwanted cases and duties of the other divisions as well as public safety. The Serenity Division is next in line for size and prestige After that, there's Narcotics, and if you're lucky enough to make the climb to the top, Homicide. From all the divisions combined, there are easily several thousand officers on duty at any given time.

I don't make it more than three feet past the bar code scanner at the entrance before Sergeant Carson sees me from across the room. His eyes widen as they meet mine.

"Havoc, my office, NOW!" he barks.

I walk across the room toward Carson's enclosed office. It reminds me of a guard box in the middle of a penitentiary cafeteria. All the other officers seated behind their smart desks avert their eyes as I pass. Edsel Carson is a heavyset white man in his late thirties, and the stress of the job has started to prematurely gray his thick black hair. I can stand Carson most days, but he hates dealing with the extra paperwork when I neglect to follow orders. He tenses up so tightly that there's a risk he'll pop all the buttons off of one of his never-changing wardrobe of white, long-sleeved, button-up shirts. Wondering who would sew those buttons back on gives me something lighter to think about than the coming conversation. Plus, I'm becoming distracted by the question of how I'm going to make this month's rent. It's almost a more alarming thought than losing Johnathan or getting in a fistfight with Harris and Metzler.

"Sit down, Havoc."

I begrudgingly inhabit the chair across from Carson's smart desk. The reflection of his face on the tilted surface of the glossy desktop fades as the whisper-quiet motors inside bring it into a horizontal position. Carson closes the door with a tap of his finger on the desk screen. He slides his index finger across the privacy icon in the lower right corner. The glass in the office windows instantly turns opaque. Now no one outside can see or hear our conversation.

"I told you specifically not to pursue Johnathan on your own, Havoc. Not only did you disobey a direct order, but now you've gone and let him shoot himself." Carson's tone is firm and condescending.

"I'm sorry, sir."

"Sorry? Jesus, Havoc, I wanted him brought in alive. He was a former officer."

"I tried to talk him down. I went after him on my own because Metzler and Harris were on duty." And because I'm feeling particularly fed up with this entire case, I add coolly, "You know they would have shot him."

"I will make the judgment calls about my own officers, Havoc. I put Metzler and Harris on this case with you because Johnathan was Metzler's old partner. If anyone could have talked him down, it would have been Metzler." Carson takes a pointed draw on his vape, then exhales a cloud of mist with a frustrated-sounding huff. "You disobeyed my order. Suicide makes the officers just as nervous as it makes the public. Now I have to find a way to make this look good for the media. Did you fire on Johnathan?"

"Yes, sir, I hit him in the shoulder when I was in pursuit."

"I take it he used his own gun to blow his brains out."

"Yes, sir."

"Did he ever aim it at you?" Carson asks, thick eyebrows raised.

"Not that I saw, sir."

He sighs, gripping the vape between his fingers almost tight enough to snap it. "We'll just have to go with the mentally unstable story." His eyes dart from side to side as if he is paging through his thoughts.

"Tonight didn't turn out the way I wanted it to either, sir."

"What is that supposed to mean?" Carson snaps.

"I was hoping to bring him in. I haven't met quota yet this month," I say, watching for his reaction.

"You're one of the more trustworthy officers in this department because you don't go trying to meet full quota all the time. I got notification that you brought in a Techie. That should help pay the bills."

"It isn't enough."

Carson leans back in his chair, folding his arms over his chest. "If you're having money problems, you should've come to me instead of trying to solve them on your own. I can help you find ways to meet quota and still keep your principles."

He sounds almost as if he's concerned about me, but I'm not fooled. The sentiment is hollow. "Thank you, sir."

"Let's be clear on this Johnathan mess. Since there's nothing better to say, I'm going to tell the media the truth. He was a troubled ex-officer, and he accidentally killed his wife in an altercation. Officers were sent in pursuit of him, and he took his own life in the process. If anyone asks, send them to Libros. Do you understand?"

Jamie Libros is the department's lead human relations officer, with a notorious reputation for never responding to messages and a knack for giving vague, noncommittal replies to any question she's asked. Her duties are so divorced from facts that her job title is meant merely to appease the often-offended masses with the idea that we're "taking care of things."

"Johnathan set that Techie on me, sir. He told him to kill me."

Carson groans, and another plume of vapor streams out of his nostrils. "The last thing I need right now is people freaking out about Techies running around with murder on the brain. When you write your report, keep that out of it."

"Yes, sir."

"Good. Now, report to the Narcotics sergeant first thing in the morning. I'll let her know you're going to be there. She has a big bust on a Tech cartel set up for tomorrow; lots of criminals involved. It's a way for you to make quota."

"Thank you, sir."

He slides his finger across the privacy icon again and the glass walls become clear. I leave his office and then the station. Though I don't agree with Carson's choice to downplay Adams's actions, it isn't unexpected. In this screwed-up world, there's a big difference between reality and what people want to hear. A suicidal cop and a rogue druggie are nothing Motor City can't swallow, but if you connect the two of them, people will get scared. This way, Johnathan and Adams's stories will quickly disappear from the public eye.

I have other things to consider. The takedown of a Tech cartel will be dangerous. Killing either Johnathan or Adams would've been a faster route to meeting quota without getting myself killed. Metzler or Harris would have preferred that outcome.

For me, it's more complicated.

My moral code makes Motor City more difficult to navigate. She's a place better suited for those with ethical ambiguity and a taste for violence. When you're trying to keep your head low and your hands clean, she's a minefield.

CHAPTER 2

DRAB MORNING

When the alarm on my transponder goes off the following morning, I snap back from the warm oblivion of sleep into my cold, harsh reality. I'm disheartened that I only slept a few hours in the whole night. Worse, I forgot to turn the heat up before bed, leaving the room to become chilly. The sun's vivid burnt-yellow rays are pushing through the curtains, reinforcing my need to get up. I drag myself out from under the cozy pile of quilts, well worn by decades of use. They were one of my sister's better discoveries at the local secondhand store. I stretch as I rise, my feet meeting the cold, splintery surface of the centuries-old wood flooring. I wash up in the black-and-white-subway-tiled bathroom and use a dab of hair-off cream to clean my face. I begrudgingly get dressed and make the bed before leaving my room.

Different day, same routine.

Most officers pay little attention to their appearance. With the tattoo on the side of our heads, it's obvious what we are, so why bother hiding behind a uniform? Still, I think it's important to be at least somewhat formal, even if no one else does. Some might call me old fashioned, but I think it's polite to wear a nice shirt and tie. I keep my face clean-shaven and my hair slicked back. The world around me is chaos, but at least I can control myself—a small satisfaction.

The three-story Victorian house I live in with my younger sister, Rina, is almost twice the age of my Cadillac. It was last modernized during the early 2020s in one of Motor City's attempts to bring herself back from abandonment. Now, more than few decades later, there is hardly enough room left in the city for homes of its kind.

In its heyday, there were several dozen homes like it in the neighborhood. Now our home and three others are flanked by apartment buildings ten stories high. Most of the old blocks were torn down in favor of such apartments. The fact that this old house is still here is as surprising as the fact that I continue to return to it each night. It has been updated with several new amenities since its last major overhaul, and the newest bits feel tacked on and out of place. Beyond the house's ancient architecture, the area's only other real tie to the past is one large oak tree that has clung to life in its inhospitable environment. It sits between my property and the neighbor to the left, looming over our sparse lawns in an attempt to steal some sun from the vast buildings that take up most of the horizon.

When I walk into the kitchen, I find that my sister has already rehydrated us a meal. Rina is slightly shorter than I am, making her tall for a woman. Her hair is shoulder length and dirty blonde, and currently streaked with red dye. Her skin is even lighter than mine, almost like porcelain. She is on the stout and muscular side. Her physical and mental strength gives me a sense of solidarity with her; her haphazard fashion choices remind me of the rebellious way I used to dress when I was her age. I am thankful that she is so strong, but it doesn't remove my fear for her safety, only dilutes it.

Her university books are stacked on the edge of the old kitchen table. She's transfixed by the pages of the one open in front of her. A personal transponder would be a more modern tool for her studies, but books are cheaper. With rent being top on the priority list, I can't imagine what it would look like to be able to provide her with such a convenience. So she settled for her books and a primitive touch screen cell phone. Seeing her have to make do with these minimal materials almost makes me wish I had killed Johnathan. Almost.

"How's school going?" I ask.

"Good," Rina replies absently. I can tell that she barely heard me.

"You need a ride to school before I go to the station?"

Rina looks up from her book with annoyed yet amused eyes. Her ID badge next to her notebook states that she is twenty-three, but her steely, street-smart, knowing gaze says she is at least three times that. Her reply is kind but a little mocking.

"I can take myself to school, big brother."

"Yeah, I know that, I was just offering."

"I'm going to take the Fastrack over to campus," Rina says.

The Fastrack stop is only a few blocks from our home, but her being alone on the street for any distance will always worry me. I raise my hands slightly in surrender. "I only want to make sure you get there in one piece."

"I get that, but I don't plan on falling apart between here and the Fastrack stop," Rina says, rolling her eyes.

"You know what I mean. Sheesh. Go ahead and be independent then. I can't stop you."

She smiles at this. Despite the shithole of a world we live in, at least the two of us watch out for each other now. Not that long ago, our back-and-forth banter was fueled more by distrust than appreciation for one another. Once Rina settled in at Motor City State University, her moods evened out. Having a solid direction to move forward in has given her a reason to side with me more often. As soon as she saw a future for herself, her drive shifted toward getting a degree instead of taking out her frustrations on me.

I sit down across the table from her and eat what I can of the rehydrated eggs and bacon, adding salt and pepper help to mask the stale taste. I smell fresh coffee in the pot, but there isn't enough for us both to have a cup. I decide to save it for Rina. I can get some from a kiosk at work later. After I finish eating, Rina closes her book and looks at me with curiosity in her eyes.

"You do anything interesting last night?"

"I've told you a thousand times not to ask, but you always do," I say, slightly annoyed by her relentless curiosity.

"Yep, always. Besides, you woke me up at two in the morning when you came in. That's hardly enough sleep for a school night, so I want details. Something for my trouble." Rina sits back in her chair, locking eyes with me.

I've got to tell her something exciting or she won't drop the subject. Still, I try to stall. "Why should you care what happens in the department? You're studying so you can test out of a career in law enforcement."

My attempt at deflection is not effective. Her posture doesn't change, and she keeps staring at me. I run a hand through my hair. I don't want to cave in, but there's little chance of diverting her from the topic now.

"Fine. I got in late last night because I was after Johnathan Matthews."

"Really? That ex-cop that was on the news for killing his wife yesterday?" Rina asks, her expression now bemused.

"Yeah, that one."

"Did he do it?" she asks, leaning toward me on the edge of her seat.

"Yeah."

"Did you kill him?"

"No, he took his own life."

She leans back, a sigh of relief escaping her. "Wow, that's a real mess."

"Yeah, it was. I tried to talk him down, but it didn't do any good."

Rina bites her lower lip. She can always tell when something is bothering me. I wish I had as easy a time guessing when something is bothering her. Often, her stoic demeanor leaves me wondering. She turns her head slightly, eyebrows raised. "Did you want to kill him?"

"No, of course not." I look at the pile of used, dog-eared schoolbooks. Most have dicks drawn on the pictures inside. Some have stains that I don't care to know the origin of. "We could've used the extra money, though."

Rina smiles at me. It always makes me feel like a better person than I think I am. Then she shrugs and tilts her head. "There're always more crooks in this town," she says bitterly.

The implications hurt, but they're true. This is the hand we've been dealt, and we have to make the best of it. She sees my thoughts written across my tired face. "You're good at your job for the right reasons," she says reassuringly.

Rina finishes her breakfast and packs up her books. I consider mentioning my run-in with Ray Adams, but I decide not to bother her with it. I doubt she would be able to sleep at night if I told her about every close call I have in a given week. I can barely sleep with the knowledge myself.

She walks me out to the old hearse and gives me a hug before heading off in the direction of the Fastrack stop. Since any goodbye has the potential to be our last, we try to make an extra effort to have pleasant departures.

I climb into Elli, and the updated ID scanner I installed in her takes a reading of the bar code ID on the left side of my head. Her soothing voice greets me with a "Hello, Harvey," and the green LED comes on in the dash. I put the key into the ignition to start her up.

I pull out the antiquated choke knob. For the first several cranks, nothing happens. *This is exactly how I want to start the freaking day.* As if she hears my thoughts, Elli roars to life and emits a plume of white smoke from her throaty side pipes. I mutter "Thank you" under my breath. It's almost impossible to find new parts for a car this old. In a few months, or perhaps a year, I will have to pull out the engine and rebuild it on my own. An expensive prospect, but still cheaper than taking her to a refab shop to be overhauled. There are just as many refab companies now as there used to be automotive manufacturers in the early twentieth century. As Adams pointed out during his Tech-crazed delirium, such businesses have put Motor City back on the map.

There is no easy parking for Elli at the station this time. I suppose it's better that way in the long run. Carson hates it when I park out front; something about a hearse giving the department a bad reputation. I think of how many times I've held my tongue to keep from telling him what really gives the department a bad name. I find a space a block over. The smart meter scans my plate after I lock up. An annoying beep indicates that it has been recognized and the appropriate funds have been callously removed from my account.

I use the side entrance closest to the Narcotics Division. Located down the alley between the department and the neighboring high-rise, it's seldom cleaned as well as the main entryway. The lack of care has left it with the aroma of piss and cigarette smoke from thousands of nervous officers over the last few decades. As with my own home, the modern technology provided by LED signage and interactive touch screens on almost every door in sight seem out of place when paired with the older building.

I've seen some of the old twentieth-century films set in what was, to the people back then, the future, and by comparison, the world we live in is underwhelming. No fancy hover cars or ray guns, just a massive population increase and enough advances in technology to keep the world running. Even the old motto of the police has gone by the wayside. Instead of "To protect and serve," now the slogan is "Work for your city, protect your future." As if good health care and a fucking transponder make up for turning us into city-sanctioned executioners. In many ways, I think we have gone backward.

It's always a good idea to remember who you can trust in this city. That goes double for who you can trust in the department. I worked under Sergeant Riley Mitchell for the first few months of my service. I feel more comfortable about going to speak with her than I've ever felt speaking to Carson. She's one of the most upstanding individuals in the MCPD, and she has little patience for anything beyond a job done quickly and by the book. I can understand her insistence on this, as the mortality rate in her division is the highest of the whole MCPD. Officers who work full time in Narcotics can expect to survive between three and six months. For that reason, most who serve in the Narcotics Division only do so on a part-time basis, though all new officers are required to serve at least one month. It's a trial by fire tactic; if you make it under Mitchell's command, you might survive the city long enough to become an asset to the MCPD.

The door to Mitchell's office is closed, the glass opaque. Unlike the open cattle pen that is the Serenity Department, Narcotics only has a few dozen offices, a large meeting room, and a lab. The officers who serve here don't need a desk. Either they're out on the streets or six feet under the damp Michigan dirt. I press the com button. "Sergeant Mitchell, Officer Havoc reporting for duty."

There's a slight delay before her voice buzzes back at me. "Door's unlocked, Havoc. Come in."

Inside the office, she looms behind the raised screen of her smart desk, distracted. It's lit and tilted slightly toward her, though with the privacy tint feature turned on, I can't see what she's working on. I seat myself and wait for her to be finished.

Once done typing, she takes off her reading glasses and puts them in the desk drawer beside her. The smart desk's screen moves to a horizontal position and goes dark. Mitchell, who is probably in her midforties, has a chiseled, strong-featured face and a stylish haircut. Her sharp suit does a good job of concealing the bulletproof vest she is rarely seen without. Though only officers in the field are required to keep the hair shaved over their tattoos, Mitchell's bar code and name tattoo are distinguishable under her short blonde hair.

"I had a call late last night from Sergeant Carson." Her accent is faintly British. I've often wondered about her youth as an officer in London and why she chose to come to Motor City, of all places, but she's notoriously tight-lipped when it comes to personal information. "He notified me that you would be coming over this morning to assist in our next assignment."

"Yes, that's correct."

Her piercing green eyes scan my face and note my posture with the precision of a machine. Her opinion of me formed, her words are calculated.

"I took the liberty of reading your file this morning. You've done well to keep a low profile as an officer since you last worked under my command. I find it odd that you would ask to be involved in an operation of this nature so close to the end of your service. Do you mind explaining that to me?"

I nod. "That's a fair question, sergeant, but I don't think you want to hear the answer."

"I'll be the judge of that. Speak plainly, Havoc," Mitchell says unflinchingly.

"Since you've read my file, you know I don't often make as much bounty as an ordinary officer."

"And last night's pursuit ended in a suicide?"

"Yes, that's correct, sergeant. No one made a bounty off Johnathan. The Techie I booked last night has been my only take-in so far this month, ma'am."

Mitchell shakes her head. "I've been a part of this station for almost twenty years, long before the mandatory three-year service was first enforced. I can tell you from personal experience that it's ill advised to take chances like this if you want to live through your term."

"I understand that."

"Good. I am putting a note in your file that I've made the danger of this operation clear to you and you've agreed to complete your assignment despite the risk. Do you concur?"

"Yes."

"Please sign to that effect."

The signature screen comes up on the desktop in front of me. Mitchell points at it with her index finger. As I sign, it simultaneously scans my fingerprint and checks my pulse rate. A small ID pod on the wall to my left scans the bar code on the side of my head in final confirmation.

"All right, Havoc, I'll fill you in on the details." Mitchell touches the "Close" button on the desk screen, and the office's privacy glass turns opaque.

"Today's operation is to take out a small drug cartel on the east side of town," she continues. "Our intelligence suggests we are looking at an offshoot of one of the larger distributors of Tech in the Blue Orchid District, though we aren't sure which one they are affiliated with yet. You'll be on a team with nine other officers, divided into five units."

"What's the preferred method, sergeant?"

"I've been given the go-ahead for the lethal method. There are likely to be as many as thirty suspects in the building. I want a quick in-and-out operation."

"Yes, sergeant."

"Do you mind if I pair you with an inexperienced officer?"

There's only one right answer. "No."

"Good." She nods approvingly. "You'll be working with Officer Ryker Ramirez, then. He's a first-year. I've already sent the location and time of the bust to your transponder. You and Ramirez will meet up with the other four teams at ten at the rendezvous point indicated."

"Understood."

"I expect results, Havoc."

"You'll have them."

"Excellent. That'll be all. You can see yourself out." Mitchell nods curtly. I am dismissed.

Once free of the sergeant's office, I review the information she has sent me on my transponder, then go find Officer Ramirez. He stands apart from the other, jaded Narcotics officers in the meeting room, his optimistic air setting him apart even more. He has clean-cut hair and is wearing a cheap white button-down shirt with inexpensive slacks and shoes. His skin is a light bronze, and he appears to be a few inches shorter than I am. I notice that his sidearm is not secured in its holster.

"Ramirez?" I call.

His eyes dart over me; his body shifts away from me slightly. When I raise my hand for him to shake, his grip is soft and his hand shaky.

"I'm Harvey Havoc. Looks like we're paired up today."

He raises his eyebrows but quickly catches on. "Oh, right."

"You want to get a cup of coffee before we head out? There's plenty of time for it. We aren't on for another hour and a half."

"Sure, that'd be great," Ramirez says.

He takes his jacket from the chair behind one of the large round tables that fill the room and throws it over his shoulder as we make our way out of the building. He walks with long strides to keep up with my steady pace.

"You check your sidearm recently?" I ask as we walk.

"Huh?

"It isn't secured."

He looks at me wide-eyed, then fumbles to secure the snap of his holster.

"You have a car, Ramirez?"

"No."

"Mind if we take mine, then?"

"No."

As we walk the one block to the old Cadillac, I note that Ramirez is following me closely, indicative of our training to keep close to the officers around you in most cases; usually, there's a higher degree of safety when you have each other's back.

It isn't until we're right in front of the hearse that he makes the connection. He stops short. "This is yours?"

"Yeah, that's right."

He's no longer paying attention to his surroundings. He leans away from me and bumps into a passerby.

"Watch it!" the man snaps.

Ramirez says a belated "Sorry" as the man disappears into the crowd. After my first five minutes with him, I can see he has a lot to learn. If the man he bumped into had been on Tech, his lack of vigilance could have meant his demise.

"So … you're him, right?" Ramirez says, apparently unaware of his situational mistake.

"What is that supposed to mean?"

"Oh, nothing. I shouldn't have said anything," he says hastily, looking up at the cloudy sky as if he's preparing to try to distract me by discussing the weather.

I'm not letting him off the hook. "Well, you've done it now, Ramirez. Who am I to you?"

"It isn't who you are to me, Havoc. It's just that you're kind of well-known in the department."

"For what?"

He shifts his weight from one foot to the other, unable to keep still. "I … I'm not sure I should say. I don't want you to get the wrong impression of me."

I lean against the side of the hearse, still facing Ramirez. A bead of sweat rolls down his face. His hands are firmly buried in his pockets.

"It won't have an effect on my impression of you. I've heard them all." At this point, I'm much more concerned about his actions than his words.

"All what?"

"Nicknames. Rumors. Take your pick."

"Oh." He considers this. "I guess that makes sense."

"What did you hear about me that's making you so nervous, Ramirez?"

He pauses, biting his lip. The awkward silence drags on. Finally, he says, "They call you the Wanna-Be Reaper."

"Yep, I've heard that one before," I nod.

"Just officers being crass, that's all it is," Ramirez says defensively.

"True, but it's important that we're open enough to trust each other today, Ramirez. So you should say whatever is on your mind and get it over with, even if you think it's crass or disrespectful."

He shifts uncomfortably again. "Well … I heard a few officers say it's because you hardly ever kill anybody; because you drive the hearse; because your partners always get killed instead of your mark, but you always survive."

Unfortunately, I am unsurprised. "Yeah, I've definitely heard that all before. Go ahead and hop in. We can dispel your fears on the way to coffee."

He hesitates again, then goes around to the other side of the hearse. I get in and unlock the door for him as the ID scanner clears me. Once he's in the car, the warning light on the touch screen mounted on the dash begins to flash.

"Try to stay still, Ramirez. The scanner in this old girl is kind of touchy."

He remains as motionless as possible, but the warning light doesn't stop flashing. I give the side of the screen a rap with the back of my hand. The contact knocks it into submission, and it accepts his information. The warning light on the touch screen changes to yellow as I input my fingerprint to authorize adding Ramirez to the acceptable occupant file.

He looks around the inside of the hearse, clearly awestruck. "I don't think I've ever been in a car this old before. Most of the repro cars you see around are late seventies to early 2000s. My half-sister has an old car, but it's a few years newer than this."

I regard Elli with exasperated fondness. "She can be a real pain in the ass to keep maintained, but she's never let me down."

I fire up the engine. Ramirez scoots back a few inches in his seat, moving himself away from the sound.

"Don't forget to put on your seat belt," I advise. "They aren't automatic."

He fumbles with the belt as I pull out, trying to get the buckle to fasten. "Are any of the rumors about you true?"

"Well, yeah, I guess. In a way. I do barely make quota most of the time."

"What about the partner thing?"

"I haven't been partnered up all that often, to be honest," I admit. "I've lost a few partners over my time with the department, but no more than any other officer, I would think."

I pull over at an automated Super K coffee kiosk. The line is only a few cars long. I can see the face of the driver in front of us in his rear-view mirror. When the large hearse pulls up behind him, his eyes narrow and his face clenches up. He then proceeds to carefully maneuver his early 2030s Ford sedan out of the lineup.

"Does that sort of thing happen often?" asks Ramirez with an amused expression.

I let a slight smirk cross my lips as I reply. "Yeah. One of the perks of driving an old hearse, I guess."

After the automated kiosk scans my plate, it logs into my onboard screen. Ramirez and I place our order. A few minutes later, we're at the kiosk to receive our coffee. It takes me a while to merge back into the heavy traffic. On the main road again, I begin to head across town toward the rendezvous point.

"You've got plenty of ammo on you, right?" I ask.

Ramirez glances in his jacket pocket, I assume to be sure he has a few spare clips. He takes out his sidearm and slips out the magazine. After a quick glance, he reloads his gun, careful to aim it away and down as he does this. It's the most responsible action I have seen him take so far.

"Yeah, I have plenty," he says.

"There's extra in the glove box, too. Go ahead and take some."

He opens the glove box and takes a few more clips, carefully placing them in his jacket. "You got plenty too?" he asks.

"Yeah. Mine takes a different caliber than the department issue, though."

"What do you use?"

".50 Magnum with modified fingerprint ID."

"Jesus, they have no business calling you the Wanna-Be Reaper. That's practically a cannon." Ramirez sounds impressed.

"It's overkill, but I hardly need more than one bullet to get the job done. Mostly I just scare the shit out of people with it. That leads to more nonviolent takedowns."

Ramirez considers this, then says, "Havoc, can I ask you something?"

"Shoot."

"How do you do it?"

"What?"

"Survive."

It takes me a minute to decide how to respond. I haven't had a partner in months, and motivational speeches are not my forte. "There's no special secret to it, Ramirez. Honestly, I've been lucky."

"You're almost three years in. It has to be more than luck."

"I haven't died, true. That doesn't mean I've been lucky all the time."

"What are your on-duty injuries?" Ramirez asks.

"I've been shot four times. Two of them were on my first day. In my first year of service, a Techie stabbed me three times because her buddy dared her to. Other than that, I've only had a few broken bones."

He shakes his head, impressed. "I haven't had any injuries yet."

"Then you're luckier than me, Ramirez."

"I guess." He shrugs. "It feels like that just means when I do get hurt, it'll be serious."

He clearly needs a pep talk, whether it's my forte or not. "Look, Ramirez, the best method of survival in this city is common sense. If you act smart and stay calm, you can get out of most situations. Even the bad ones."

"What about the other situations, the really dangerous ones, like today?" His voice is pitched slightly higher. He darts a glance at me.

"Think about where you are right now, Ramirez," I say matter of factly. "You are in a hearse. We are on our way to a big drug bust in one of the most dangerous cities in America. Everybody dies at some point."

"Is that supposed to make me feel better?"

"It's supposed to make you think. You're alive right now. Enjoy that. Don't be afraid of dying. It's something that happens to everybody at some point. Fear makes you screw up; it makes you more vulnerable."

"So your secret is that you're fearless?" He sounds dubious.

"I'm scared every day, Ramirez. Who isn't? That doesn't mean I let it control how I do things. See past the fear. Try to stay calm and confident." I sound so convincing, I almost believe myself.

37

CHAPTER 3

BUST

We're only few miles from the department when the traffic gets thick enough to bring us to a standstill. I peer out of Elli's vast windshield at the sea of cars ahead. Horns honk, and I hear the occasional expletive from various people frustrated with their time-related predicaments. Ramirez sits quietly on the bench seat beside me. I decide to pass the time by testing his knowledge.

"How much do you know about Tech?" I ask.

"Um, the basics, I guess."

"Well, run through what you know."

"It's very dangerous, and just as addictive, too."

"And?"

"When people take it, they're incredibly impressionable." He pauses, then adds, "It's easy to overdose on if you inhale it."

"Anything else?" I ask. His answers so far are at least fifty percent wrong. Plus, I've never heard of someone inhaling Tech; that isn't how it works. *This is not a good sign,* I think grimly.

"I don't know. I've been too busy trying not to get killed to think about it much."

"Not knowing about Tech is a good way to get killed, man." I let out a frustrated sigh. "You understand why people take it, right?"

"It makes them feel good, I guess? I don't really know."

"It's because it makes them feel nothing," I correct him. "All their problems go away, and they forget pain, anger, everything."

"How do you know?" Ramirez asks.

"I talk to the expert on such matters, Tek."

"Wait, I'm confused. You talk to the drug about the drug?"

"No, Tek is the nickname of the department narcotics expert, Anteka Sokola. Have you ever talked to her?"

"No."

I glance over at the dash screen and see that it's just after nine. I could try to give Ramirez a full briefing on Tech, but no one knows more than Sokola. Going into a bust with a rookie who has this little knowledge of Tech is as dangerous for me as it is for Ramirez. Our survival over the next few hours is far more important than the time we'll lose going back to the station.

"Hold on," I say, flipping on the hidden lights and siren before he has the chance to protest.

The vehicles around us haphazardly move to make way. More horns and expletives erupt as I maneuver Elli through the parting cars. Once headed in the other direction, I put my foot down as traffic gets a little lighter. Ramirez desperately holds onto the dashboard and the armrest in an attempt to stabilize himself as I weave the big hearse in and out of traffic.

We make it back to the department in half the time we'd taken to go get coffee. Out front, I see a nicely placed, albeit narrow, spot to park Elli and screech the hearse into it. Ramirez transfers his free hand to the dash, bracing himself as all three tons of vehicle come to a loud and abrupt stop.

"What the hell was that all about? We have to be at the rendezvous point in forty-five minutes," Ramirez says, catching his breath.

"If I'm going into this bust with you, then you're going to meet Tek first."

Ramirez raises both eyebrows in concern; however, the topic is not up for debate. We climb out, and I lock up before we head in. We need to make this quick. Carson will be pissed if I leave Elli out front for too long. We head past the Narcotics Division meeting room and offices, toward the back corner of the building.

I stop by an in-wall Super K coffee kiosk outside the Narcotics break room. I call up an order on the screen for the largest coffee I can buy, with white chocolate and coconut flavoring.

"What are you doing? We still have coffee in the car," Ramirez asks with narrowed eyes.

"Peace offering."

Though he looks at me in anticipation of further explanation, I ignore him and head to the end of the hall. The on-site Narcotics lab is home to our person of interest. The door's mesh-reinforced glass is vibrating with the deep bass of the rap playing over Tek's stereo. Ramirez shields his ears with his palms as we enter. The music is far too loud for her to notice us at first.

Anteka is possibly the most colorful officer in the department. She's under five feet tall, and her almost childlike stature complements her bold and bubbly personality. The bright streaks of neon red in her shoulder-length black hair stand out against her fair skin. The white of her lab coat is marred by an array of offbeat patches with slogans such as "Death to all who don't bring me coffee." Someone who doesn't know her well might think the best word to describe her is "cute."

She *is* cute; she also happens to be delightfully crass and borderline psychotic. I think half the reason they gave her a desk job in the force was to keep the streets from running as red as the streaks in her hair. She finally catches sight of us, startled only slightly by our stealthy entry. She lowers the sound by uttering a command of "Shut up!" to the lab's interactive sound system.

"Harvey!" she exclaims.

Tek is one of the only people in this place to call me by my first name. I hold out the massive coffee and give her a modest bow with my greeting. "Tek, how've you been?"

"Same day, different shit, you know. Oooh, coffee," Anteka says, grasping the cup with both hands.

"Got a newbie here for you to drop some knowledge on about your favorite subject."

"Oh, you mean the super drug," she states, as though it's normal for a person's favorite subject to be Tech.

Tek looks Ramirez up and down. A devilish grin makes its way across her deceptively innocent face. She releases one small hand from the coffee for Ramirez to shake. He glances briefly in my direction with wild eyes before shaking her hand.

"Anteka Sokola at your disposal. You can call me Tek if you like. Or don't, if it confuses you."

"Ramirez. Nice to meet you," he replies feebly.

"How much time we got, Harvey?" Tek asks, one eyebrow raised.

"We're due to be part of that big bust today at ten, so not a lot."

"Right, I'll try for the short version, then: Shit you need to know so you don't get your ass killed."

Ramirez nods, and I lean back against a nearby counter. The lab is cramped because of all the equipment crammed into it, but well-lit by a vast array of overhead and spot lighting. Anteka only has a few part-time assistants, and none of them are here at the moment. The stainless steel counters are covered in an array of instruments that I have no clue how to use. There's a large aquarium behind her with a freakishly oversized goldfish in it. The lab cat, a lazy calico named Delilah, has perched herself on a counter adjacent to the aquarium and is watching intently as the fish swims back and forth. I get the impression once that cat figures out how to break into the fish tank, the world will be her oyster.

"I'm going to go with the assumption that you don't know shit about any of this," Tek says. Ramirez's blank look confirms her suspicions, so she dives right in. "The first version of Tech came out around thirty years ago. It's an amazing synthesis of opioids, amphetamines, benzos, cocaine, and a buttload of other chemicals. Mainly, the components are of the pharmaceutical variety, but the versions more common on the streets have the added allure of being made in the ghetto with chemicals such as toilet cleaner, battery acid, and nail polish remover. Usually gives off a delightful odor similar to Delilah here taking piss in an uncleaned litter box."

Anteka pauses to sip her coffee. Ramirez takes a deep breath, as if he thinks it's over, but I know better.

"It's an extreme upper and downer, so it actually ends up equalizing your body and mind to a seminormal level, but it gives you a much higher high and a much lower low," Tek continues. "So you're stuck in this comfortably numb zone where you're entirely neutral and indifferent; it overloads the senses so completely that you don't really feel anything. The cocaine and amphetamines would normally send your ass into cardiac arrest, and the opioids would overload the opioid receptors in your brain, which would interrupt the signals regulating your breathing and cause respiratory arrest. However, by mixing them, you get the high from the uppers and the low from the downers without overdosing."

She takes another big gulp of coffee. This time, Ramirez holds his breath.

"It's the same thing bored, overachieving, suburban soccer moms do with Xanax and Adderall, albeit on a much less potent scale. That's why it's called a Suburban Speedball. There are plenty of functional Techies in society, probably some right here in this police department. So don't be lulled into the false assumption that it's only losers who are drooling on themselves in the streets that are on it, unless you're looking to get yourself killed."

She takes a short breath this time—no coffee chugging—then plunges ahead.

"In small doses, it doesn't cause addiction, and you'd get physically dependent long before you got addicted. You know, one of the things I had to do to qualify for this job was take a controlled dose of it. When they gave it to me, my handler told me to meow like a cat. I did that for two straight hours before it wore off, which is about the normal amount of time Tech's effects last. We all know that to truly understand something, you have to experience it. And we all know that one controlled dose isn't nearly enough to really experience it. So for the sake of not getting my ass in trouble, we'll say that I know the effects firsthand from that one experience, and everything else, I've learned from mice and goldfish. Not just this goldfish, either. Sometimes I go over to Booking and talk to the Techies that they bring in. They're my other goldfish."

She pauses to take the biggest swig of coffee yet. Ramirez is in information overload. He's swaying on his feet, as if a slight breeze could knock him over.

"Anyway, you don't really have feelings when you've been on it for a while, because you're used to the heightened senses and it just makes you feel normal. So if something stands in your way of getting more, you'll do absolutely anything to get it, because your body will go into withdrawal otherwise. It's kind of like the old idea of zombies. You become an impressionable zombie version of yourself on it, but you go running around in search of Tech instead of brains. Off of it, you become a violent, desperate, empty shell. The amphetamine component causes you to go into a hyperfocused state, so if someone plants a thought in your mind within the first hour it's in your system, you obsessively focus on it."

"Holy shit," Ramirez says, propping himself up against the nearest counter.

"You think all that's bad?" Tek says with a dismissive snort. "It gets worse. Everyone is unique, and not in a 'We're all beautiful individual snowflakes' bullshit way. Our bodies all have unique chemicals, hormones, genetics, and tolerances. So all of those factors, combined with the chemical composition of the specific strain of Tech and an ungodly amount of other science garbage, basically means that Tech fucks you up and can make anyone do anything, and there's no way to predict any of it. It can be smoked, snorted, or taken in pill form, and it's absorbed into fetuses."

Anteka points at her neon-red-streaked hair. Ramirez looks confused. "Some of the people you see walking around with odd hair colors? You can thank Tech for that. It's been known to cause mutations in unborn children. The current thought is that the laser tattoo process designed to alter your DNA so it changes your skin color is where that comes from. Somehow, the altered skin cells can be transmuted by the Tech and transferred to the kid in utero. Fuck if I know how that's possible, because it shouldn't be, but I've heard a lot of theories. Anyway, in my case, my mother had a tattoo with red and black ink. Ta-da, I get red and black hair because my mom was a Techie."

On finishing her speech, Tek smiles brightly and sips from her cup of coffee.

Ramirez falls backward onto a nearby stool, which provides better support than the counter. "How the hell are we supposed to deal with something like that?" he asks, eyes wide and despondent.

"Well, now you know more than half the population cares to know. That's a step in a direction. I think the answer is kind of simple, though: Don't trust anyone." Tek says this without losing her smile.

Ramirez and I thank Anteka for her time and head back out to the hearse. It's just after nine thirty. I turn on the lights and siren as we pull out. Ramirez is in a justifiable daze from all the information that's been dumped on him. He remains distant on the fast-paced ride to the other side of town. Despite my erratic driving, he does not brace himself as before; instead, he stares out the window and watches as we pass people by. No doubt he's seeing the sea of possible Tech zombies for the first time.

I shut down the sirens and lights a few blocks before arriving at the rendezvous point. There are no other officers or squad cars in the area yet. A glance at the dash screen tells me it's about twenty to ten. Sergeant Mitchell selected a good location. The mostly empty parking lot is within walking distance of the target building. It's in the shadow of enough surrounding structures that no one will immediately notice us congregating here. I drive Elli to the far side of the lot, concealing my odd vehicle by parking it behind an old panel van with two long-since-flat tires.

"You know any of the other officers on this team, Ramirez?" I ask.

"Most of them regularly volunteer in the Narcotics Division except you and two others."

"Let me guess, Metzler and Harris."

"Yeah."

I shut off the engine and turn my gaze to Ramirez. "My advice is to keep your distance from them, Ramirez. Those two are bad news."

"That's what I heard, too. How'd you suppose they got in on this operation?"

"Probably the same way I did. They asked. I take it you were selected?"

"Yeah. Mitchell said I need the experience. I'm the freshest in this operation." He doesn't sound happy.

"Seriously, Ramirez, don't think about it too much. It might be a dangerous job, but it will be over soon. Besides, now you know a lot more about what you're getting into."

"I guess. Is all that stuff about Tech that Sokola was talking about true?"

"Yeah, unfortunately it is."

There's little point in more conversation as we gather the gear from the back of my hearse. I have given Ramirez all the advice I can. The rest is up to him to find out on his own. His eyes light up when I pull out extra body armor and a shotgun he can borrow. The department doesn't provide as high a quality of gear as you can find in the private market. After you've seen a bullet go right through a department-issue vest, you find a way to get your own in a hurry.

"How'd you get all this stuff?" he asks.

"I don't make much money. What I do make, I invest wisely."

We finish our now disappointingly cool coffee as we wait for the rest of the team, sitting side by side on the wide rear bumper of the Cadillac. The city is quiet this early in the morning. All of the degenerates are still in bed with a hangover from last night. I hear the hum of the nearby power station a few blocks over. Farther down an alley at the other end of the parking lot, a cat fight breaks out. A cool morning breeze carries the smell from the nearby river. Ramirez breaks the relative silence after a time, pointing at the sticker in the middle of the hearse's back window.

"What does that mean?"

I glance back at the sticker, an old-fashioned tombstone in white with a black border. A skull with wings graces the top, and crossed bones on either side provide embellishment. The words beneath the winged skull read "Memento Mori."

"It means 'Remember that you will die,' or 'Remember your mortality,' whichever you like."

Ramirez doesn't reply; instead, he stares off into the distance. I can't blame him for his reaction. I'm not sure why the saying gives me comfort. After more awkward silence passes, I hear the loud whistle of a turbocharged engine in the distance. A few moments later, a highly modified early 2000s red Porsche pulls in. I recognize Metzler and Harris through the lightly tinted glass. Some kind of obnoxious techno-rap is blasting inside. They park as far from us as they can, get out, and begin to gear up. I can't decide which one of them looks more comical. I nudge Ramirez's shoulder with my own.

"Looks like Beetle and McMustache are here."

Ramirez and I chuckle softly at my remark.

Over the next few minutes, the remaining three teams of officers show up. It appears to be a veritable who's who from all four of the MCPD divisions. This ragtag crew of street cops, detectives, and rookies must share my money problems to have volunteered for such an assignment, though Harris and Metzler are no doubt also along for the glory of more kills. Ramirez seems to be the only one who didn't ask to be here. The other teams gear up, and then we all wait with transponders in hand. At precisely ten o'clock, Mitchell's face comes onto our screens so she can deliver a final briefing.

"My scanner check indicates that all ten of you are present and in good shape," she says crisply. "Are all of you wearing your tactical gear?"

"Yes, sergeant," rings out from all of us, almost in unison.

"Good. I want a clean, fast operation. We're looking at a variety of suspects with a full range of weapons and explosives. Shoot to kill order. If it moves, this is its last day. I expect each and every one of you to report in as soon as it's done. Good luck."

Her face disappears from our transponder screens. For the next half hour or so, we are on our own; it's us against them. Keeping low, we make our way toward the target building. Ramirez keeps close to me. The others keep their distance from each other. Any drug-related situations are handled with military tactics. The unpredictable nature of Tech forced this method to become standard.

It's a large brick building, unassuming from the outside, probably some type of factory, given its proximity to the water. As we near the front of the building, Ramirez and I take cover behind a dumpster across the street. The smell of rotting meat emanating from it is unpleasant, but the protection it provides is worth it. If we weren't otherwise occupied, I would be suspicious enough to inspect its contents for the origin of the odor. Metzler and Harris make their way to the door with a small explosive device. Ramirez lets out a deep sigh, obviously glad he won't be the first one in.

I remove a pair of tactical glasses from my jacket pocket, don them, and switch them on. The world comes into detailed focus on the grid layout I see before me. The stream of data flows across the data bar at the edge of the viewing screen, almost too fast to read. A quick count confirms that there are thirty separate heat signatures in the building.

Ramirez follows suit and puts his glasses on. Then the charge Metzler placed on the door blows. The heat signatures scatter at first, then reconverge, some moving toward the front of the building. Six of these targets appear to be headed to the back, possibly making for an exit. As the rest of the team pushes through the front entrance in a hail of gunfire, I motion to Ramirez. He follows me down a side alley toward the back of the building. We keep low in case any stray gunfire makes it through the walls to our right. In the corner of the tactical glasses' screen, the two counters change. We are at two officers and five suspects down so far.

Once we're at the back door, the tactical glasses reveal that the six suspects we've been following are almost outside. Ramirez and I take cover on opposite sides of the back door and line up our shots. As the door swings open, before the chaos starts, we each manage to drop one suspect cleanly. The other four retreat into the building, but not before I hit one of them below the kneecap. Given the caliber of my gun, the shot effectively removes his leg. Before he can scream much, a shot from Ramirez puts him out of his misery. A hail of bullets erupts from the doorway and windows toward us. The other three suspects have good enough cover that our shots are not making a difference.

The suspect counter in the corner of my glasses ticks upward, adding our three kills and two more from within. The other counter is holding at two officer fatalities. I remove a grenade from a pouch on my tactical belt. Ramirez sees me throw it and ducks behind a small brick wall nearby. I brace myself as the grenade flies into the building. The explosion rocks the ground beneath me. The suspect counter rises by two, and a flashing yellow light in the corner of the lens indicates that the remaining suspect is injured. Ramirez and I move from our hiding places and over to the wreckage of the doorway.

Just inside the gaping hole where a door used to be and to our left is the remaining suspect. She's gasping desperately for air, shrapnel protruding from her gut. It appears to be a jagged splinter of wood from one of the nearby walls. I nod to Ramirez to finish the job, as I already have the three kills I need. Ramirez raises his gun, but then takes his finger off the trigger.

"Finish it, Ramirez."

"I can't, damn it! She's just a kid!"

"She's old enough to shoot at us and peddle drugs on the street. This is our job."

"I'm sorry, Harvey. I can't."

He begins to lower the gun. I holster my sidearm and grab hold of Ramirez's hand, forcing my finger into the trigger slot with his. The shot rings out in our ears. The suspect's body slumps back onto the pile of wreckage behind her. In the corner of my lens, the suspect count hits thirteen; a few seconds later, it's at fifteen. The officer count is up to three. *Damn.*

"Jesus, Harvey. Why did you make me do that?" Ramirez is aghast.

"In her condition, that was a mercy." My words taste foul.

Ramirez is frozen in place, eyes fixed on the corpse. He slowly lowers his gun again.

"Come on, Ramirez. We're three officers down. They need our help in there."

He hesitates a moment more before following me up a nearby staircase leading to the upper floors. As we reach the second-floor landing, a quick look around reveals that there are several suspects on this level. The suspect count is up to sixteen. We are now down four officers.

As we enter the hallway, the heat signatures fade from the tactical glasses' screen. After I tap the reset button on the side a few times to no avail, it becomes clear that someone has switched on a signal disrupter. This must be a well-funded drug operation to afford that level of defense against department gear. I turn to Ramirez and whisper, "We're on our own."

He nods, and we proceed down the hall, keeping low. The tactical glasses are of little use now, so we remove them. Gunshots ring out from above and below us. A few feet ahead, the hallway splits into a T. Though Ramirez is clearly unnerved by the idea, here we split up. He heads to the left; I go to the right.

The building is dimly lit and smells of mold and mildew, with a distant scent of chemicals. No doubt the Tech lab is somewhere on this floor. As I make my way down the long hallway, the chemical scent gets stronger. Hopefully this means that the direction Ramirez went was the safer one. As I advance, I feel the guilt set in. Maybe making him kill the young woman was the wrong thing to do. *I should've done it on my own and spared him the nightmares.* It's a decent thought, but obviously too little, too late.

There's a large double door to my left, and a room at the end of the hall seems to be the origin of the chemical smell, a horrid combination of ammonia, battery acid, and Drano. I put my back to the wall and edge as close to the door as I dare. I hear voices inside. There must be at least a few suspects within. I breathe deeply and prepare myself for my next move. I decide to kick the door in and advance with a spray of covering gunfire. If I keep low, I may be able to take them down without getting in their line of fire.

A single shot echoes in my ears, and pain pierces through me like a hot knife. I look down to see the white shirt under my body armor changing to red. My legs feel weak and heavy as I slip to the floor. The shot must've come through the wall. Penetrating my lower back on the right side, it missed my body armor by millimeters.

I hear footsteps running toward me from the hall I came down. I expect to see Ramirez come into view, but instead, Harris appears. He gets close, and when he notices my wound, he stops abruptly and crouches down. He speaks more softly than I have ever heard him speak before.

"Havoc, what's happened?"

"I think we have multiple targets in there. They must have a signal jammer. Our tactical glasses went out right after we came into the building."

"That'd explain it."

He takes the risk of creeping across the hall toward me. He takes a painkiller shot from a pouch beneath his body armor and injects it into my arm. I hear another set of footsteps coming closer from down the hallway. There's also a dragging sound.

I ignore this, hoping that the painkiller will set in soon. The pain only seems to be getting worse, though, so I decide to go for a shot from my own bag. To my dismay, I realize that I cannot raise my hand. A sick grin makes its way across Harris's face as he notices my efforts. *Shit.* I can't move my head either. I dart my eyes to the side. I see Metzler coming toward us, dragging someone behind him. Harris hasn't injected me with a painkiller, he's given me a paralytic. He stands up and calls through the closed double doors, "It's OK, Hal. You can open up. It's just me and Metzler."

The double doors open and a tall, thin man with glasses emerges. He's holding a gun with both hands, which are shaking violently. He surveys the situation and sees me and the body Metzler is dragging.

"What's with those two?" asks Hal.

"Don't worry your pretty little head about it, Hal. They're part of the plan." Harris takes my gun and tactical gear, then grabs my collar and drags me into the room. As he places my limp body against the other side of the wall from where I was shot, I see that there two other suspects in the room, and that the figure on the floor behind Metzler is Ramirez. Metzler drags him past me and props him up against the wall beside me. There is terror in Ramirez's wide, bloodshot eyes, and he's not moving much. It's a safe bet that he's been given the same paralytic as I have.

Hal shakily sets his gun down on the edge of a nearby table. "We weren't supposed to lose so many of the crew, Metzler."

"Yeah? Well, it isn't easy getting this kind of thing done, Hal. We've lost people on our side too."

"This wasn't the deal," Hal says grimly. Metzler glares at him.

Harris chimes in to break the tension. "Fewer men involved means each of us gets a bigger take-home, Hal."

"True, I guess." Hal shrugs. "The money is transferred. All the Tech was shipped out about an hour before you got here."

"That's excellent. What about the evidence?" asks Metzler.

"All taken care of. There's enough chemicals in these tanks to make an explosion that'll bring down this building."

Metzler smiles, pleased, as Harris asks, "Will it look like all of the drugs were destroyed in the fire?"

"Yeah. Nobody will know what happened except us," Hal says with a grin. Before he or his colleagues have a chance to react, Harris and Metzler raise their guns and shoot the three of them down. After a quick check to ensure that they're dead, Metzler and Harris turn their attention back to Ramirez and me. Metzler speaks first, glee in his voice.

"You know, Johnny boy almost fucked up this whole operation. Got cold feet at the end. I had to dose him with Tech and set him on his wife. Could've made extra for killing him, too, if you hadn't fucked up and let him off himself."

"That druggie Adams should've taken you out. Not sure how you dodged that little trap I set for you," says Harris.

I remember Anteka's words from earlier today. You have to plant an idea in a Techie's mind within the first hour of them taking the drug. There was no way Johnathan could've known when Adams had taken Tech. And he wouldn't have had the time, as he ran by, to implant the idea of killing me. Harris and Metzler must have set it up beforehand. They might even have walked me right past Adams if I'd been foolish enough to try tracking down Johnathan with them instead of on my own.

"You really should've stayed out of this operation, Havoc. Such a Wanna-Be Reaper." Harris raises my gun toward my head. In the seconds before he pulls the trigger, a dozen thoughts flash through my mind. Foremost, I realize that Rina will be stuck on her own if I die here. I also realize that the young woman I just made Ramirez kill was probably Rina's age. As Harris squeezes the trigger, I grit my teeth in preparation for the imminent end.

BANG!

The sound rings in my ears, piercing my very soul. I hate myself so much that I almost wish I hadn't installed the concealed fingerprint ID on my .50-caliber Magnum revolver. The safety feature does its job, forcing the round to explode through the back of the gun barrel and into Harris' face in a blast of fire and shrapnel.

From the corner of my eye, I see that Ramirez has regained some movement. He takes advantage of Metzler's shock and pulls his concealed sidearm from its ankle holster. Metzler will never know what hit him. He falls to the ground, dead, an expertly placed bullet hole between his beady little eyes. There is, however, an unfortunate side effect of Ramirez's skillful shot. The bullet that passed through Metzler's forehead kept going into the large chemical tank behind him.

Though the bullet doesn't ignite the flammable liquid as it enters the tank, Metzler's body knocks a small burner off of the table behind him as he falls. Ramirez and I exchange glances, both of us realizing that our time is limited. He grabs me beneath the shoulders and starts to drag me from the room. His efforts are slow and labored since the paralytic has not fully worn off. As he makes it to the hall, right before the room is out of view, I see the liquid ignite.

Ramirez is panting desperately as he drags me as fast as he can down the long hall. I want to help him, but I can barely lift a finger. *We're gonna die here.* When we're almost at the end of the hall, flames lap out of the room behind us. Ramirez doesn't look back to see our death coming. The flames erupt into a massive ball of fire and smoke, and the building shifts and splits beneath us. The ravenous flames lunge down the hall. I close my eyes and grit my teeth.

CHAPTER 4

AFTERMATH

Flashes of light are punctuated by pain. People's frantic voices surround me, but the ringing in my ears makes them sound like they're far away. This continues for an amount of time I cannot gauge. The rest of my time is spent in darkness. I prefer the darkness; it's accompanied by less pain. Eventually, I recognize Rina's voice in the background. No matter how much I make my lips quiver, no sound will escape them.

Time passes slowly. I cannot tell how long I've been like this.

I finally wake up to a sterile, brightly lit room. I'm lying on a hospital bed. I feel pressure and a dull pain in my chest. The vitals screen in the wall next to me lights up with an array of excited numbers and signals that mean little to my dazed mind. No doubt a doctor or nurse will soon arrive to check on me, though I'm surprised and a little disappointed that Rina isn't here. Instead, a man in his forties with graying brown hair is sitting in the chair opposite me.

Judging by his well-tailored dark blue suit, it would appear I'm in the presence of an elite member of the MCPD. He's clean-shaven and well groomed, his eyes a dark brown. His hair is cut short enough to show that he doesn't have a bar code tattoo. This further confirms my suspicion that I'm in the presence of a high-ranking individual. Noticing that I've awakened, he shuts down the screen of his transponder, puts it in his inner suit pocket, and directs his attention to me.

"Good to see you awake, Havoc." His voice is deep and relaxed. His face is calm, almost devoid of expression.

"I'm surprised to be awake," I say, squinting in the brightness of the room.

"You did have quite the close call. Do you know where you are?"

I take a moment to more carefully analyze the room before I reply, noticing that the fixtures and finishes are all new. Unlike civilian hospitals in the Motor City area that have been updated over many decades, the department hospital has only been in service for the last five years. Thanks to my prior on-duty injuries, its rooms are familiar to me. "The department hospital, officers only."

"Yes, Havoc. Do you remember what brought you here?"

"Yes, I do, sir."

"My name is Mark Anderson. I'm the chief of the Motor City Police Department."

It seems condescending of him to spell it out like that, as if I wouldn't recognize the name. I pretend not to notice as I answer him. "It's good to meet you, sir."

"Do you know why I'm here, Harvey?"

"I assume it has to do with the circumstances of the bust."

He nods. "I'm sure you can understand the gravity of the situation."

"Yes, sir, I can."

"Good. If you feel up to it, I would like to discuss your options." Anderson leans back slightly, settling into his chair.

"What do you mean by that?"

"Harvey, nine officers are dead, two of whom were dirty. I, among others in the department, have questions."

My heart sinks at the realization that Ramirez and the others are dead. So many lives wasted over a few crooked cops. Anderson's right, the whole mess raises a pile of unsavory questions. "What do you want to know?"

"Did you know of Metzler and Harris's involvement prior to the bust?" Anderson has brought out his transponder again so he can take notes.

"No. I only found out when Harris used a paralytic on me."

"Do you know if any other officers were involved besides them?"

"I'm not sure. Our tactical glasses were knocked out when we entered the building. Ramirez and I were operating blind."

"I see. Who killed Harris and Metzler?"

"Harris had taken my gun before we entered the room. It has a fingerprint safety mechanism of my own design. When he attempted to shoot me, it backfired and killed him. At around that time, Ramirez regained enough control to use a concealed firearm to take out Metzler."

"Anderson nods approvingly. "All right, that matches our findings. What of the drugs?"

"Harris and Metzler were talking to one of the suspects. They called him Hal. Hal said that the drugs had been moved prior to the bust, and he pointed out that the explosion would make it look like they'd been destroyed."

"What happened after the suspects were taken down?"

"The shot that killed Metzler passed through him and ruptured a chemical tank. During his fall, he knocked a burner off of the table behind him. That started the fire."

"Then Ramirez tried to take you out of the building?"

"Yes, but the explosion put a stop to that."

This seems to be the end of Anderson's rapid-fire questions. He regards me for a moment. "Your account of the situation matches the scene investigator's, Harvey."

"Isn't that a good thing?"

The chief sighs deeply before responding, crossing his arms over his chest. "Yes and no."

"Why's that?" I ask, not really wanting to know the answer.

"There are people higher up the food chain than I am, Harvey. A dirty cop is bad publicity for the department; two dirty cops is even worse. There is concern that given your injuries, you will want to apply for an early retirement."

I think about how Metzler and Harris were involved with Johnathan. *The department obviously hasn't found out about their little confession to me. Three dirty cops for sure; who knows how many could be in on this thing?* I decide to keep this sliver of knowledge to myself for later use. You never know when you'll need a back door.

"Why should my retirement concern anyone?" I ask.

"Harvey, you have entered the realm of department politics." The chief looks as if he almost feels sorry for me. "Right now, you're seen as a hero. But if you talk too much about what happened, people could get the wrong impression."

"So what do you want from me?"

"Everyone would be more comfortable if you stayed on rather than retired."

His words and the way he's staring at me raise my hackles. "Is that a threat, sir?"

"No, Harvey, this is me giving you advice about your best possible future. Just think about it, and come see me when you're well again." With that, Anderson puts his transponder away and leaves. I notice him speaking with one of the doctors as they pass each other in the hall.

Moments later, the doctor enters. He's a thin, balding older man with skin so dark it's almost as black as the midnight sky. He's wearing rectangular-framed glasses and a clean lab coat, and holding a large, semitransparent data screen. His name tag informs me that he's Dr. Mobius Arnold. His voice is methodical and soft, with a slight accent I find out later is Kenyan, as he tells me that I've suffered numerous injuries: several fractured bones, a shot to the gut that damaged my lower intestine, and severe lung damage from smoke inhalation. Apparently I was trapped in the smoldering wreckage of the building for hours before they found me. I realize that the painkillers I'm on must be incredibly strong given that I feel only a dull pressure in my chest. Arnold explains in detail what he and his fellow doctors have done to put me back together.

Several feet of artificial intestine were grafted in to repair the damage from the gunshot. Some pins were used in my left leg, broken when a beam fell on it. There are more pins in my right arm, broken when some other part of the building collapsed on me. My lungs were too damaged to be repaired. The doctor tells me I was on a respirator for a few days before they performed a double lung transplant from an available donor. I grab the collar of my hospital gown and pull it away from my body, gazing down with morbid curiosity. The scar on my chest is not that dissimilar to the incision a mortician would make during an autopsy.

Suddenly I feel nauseous and dizzy as the weight of Arnold's words crashes down on me. He tells me I'm lucky to be alive, tells me to rest, and leaves me alone again. The clock in the bottom corner of the vitals screen says it's still midday. Hopefully, once Rina is out of class, she'll come by on her way home to see me. I fall into a light sleep with that comforting thought on my mind. I awake sometime later to the warm grip of Rina's tough hand in mine. Her face lights up when she sees me open my eyes.

"Hey, big brother," she says.

"Hey there, little sister."

"I was starting to wonder if you were ever planning on waking up." Relief is written across her face along with her smile.

"How long have I been here, Rina?" I ask, realizing that no one has told me this detail yet.

"It's been almost a month."

"I was in a coma?"

"Yeah. At first, they weren't sure you were going to come out of it," Rina says, biting her lip.

"I'm sorry about this mess."

"Don't worry about that, Harvey. You're a cop. We both knew something like this would happen eventually." Rina leans over the bed and gives me a big hug. Her warm tears fall onto my cheek. Mixing with my own, they collect and cascade down my face.

"I'm just glad I still have a big brother," Rina sobs.

"I'm glad to be here, sis."

It's another week until Dr. Arnold says I'm cleared to go home. Rina picks me up from the hospital in my hearse. The surprised looks we get comfort me; thanks to the hearse, I'm still intimidating despite my weakened physical state. It's odd to find myself in the passenger seat of the old Cadillac. Rina drives her slow and smooth. As we rumble down the unforgiving streets of Motor City toward home, I think, *This city tried to kill me again, but she failed.*

There's always tomorrow!

I ignore her whisper.

The house is a bit of a mess. I've always been the clean sibling. Rina seems ashamed of the clutter, but I assure her that I don't mind. It will be another few weeks or so before I can go back to work, and cleaning will give me something to do with my time. In a strange way, this is kind of a vacation for me. I haven't had the chance to stay home for this long in years. I went right from school and into the department, and being there for Rina and the job has left me little time for anything else.

Over the next few days, Rina tries her hand at cooking for us a few times. After she burns a rehydrated chicken dinner to a crisp, we agree that I'm better at cooking, and I gladly fall back into that routine. I take a little money from my meager savings and do some much-needed maintenance on the hearse. It's nice to get away from it all, but the memories of the bust wake me up in the middle of the night more than once. The hazard pay and time off are a mediocre reward for the mental and physical pain I continue to endure.

Over time, I heal well enough, though at first, the simplest things require a lot of effort. Regular shots of a special immunosuppressant help prevent my body from rejecting the new lungs, and soon it becomes easier to breathe normally. Decades ago, someone in my condition would have been on a drug regimen for life. The shots Dr. Arnold gives me need to be administered at regular intervals, but only for a month.

I gradually get myself into an exercise routine, taking short runs around our neighborhood every morning before Rina gets up. I try to eat heartily in order to gain weight. I lost almost thirty pounds over the course of my hospital stay. Rina and I eat breakfast and dinner together most days, and sometimes she comes home to check on me at lunch. In time, I start to feel and look like my old self again. I get Elli in top running order and update her scanner systems. The house is the cleanest it's been in years.

Once I'm healed enough, it'll be time to return to the Serenity Division, the opposite of what I want to do, since I've become used to a better life in the last few months. A visit to Dr. Arnold finally sees me cleared as being back to normal health. I arrive home to find that Rina has made me dinner and a cake as a surprise. It appears to be unburned in any way, giving me great hope for its quality.

"Wow, sis, this looks amazing."

"Thanks. I'll take credit for the meal, but I got the cake at the store on my way home from class," she admits.

"It's great, Rina."

To my well-concealed surprise, the dinner is delicious. We laugh and joke, enjoying the meal and the delightful dessert. By then, it's long past the time I should've said something about going back to work, and I've allowed myself to live the lie for too long. Telling Rina the truth would've meant believing the reality myself, and I've selfishly put my false freedom before honesty. Rina thinks I'm done as an officer. I decide to shatter the lie and her unwarranted hope.

"Listen, Rina, I didn't apply for an early retirement."

"What? You're fucking kidding me, right?"

"No."

Rina presses her lips tightly together, a mixture of fear and anger welling up in her eyes. "Why not, Harvey?"

I sigh deeply. I'm unwilling to tell her the rest of the truth, but she deserves to hear it. "The chief came to see me while I was in the hospital. He advised me against it."

"Who fucking cares? You almost died!" Rina yells, rising from her chair, one fist pounding on the table.

I raise my hands in protest, motioning her back down. She reluctantly sinks back into her chair. "I know, but it isn't so simple. There's more to the bust than you know about, Rina, and if I retire, it might cause trouble for us."

"Why?" she asks, glaring deep into my eyes.

"If I want to keep us safe, I need to go back."

"So they've got dirt on you?"

"No, they don't. The chief implied that some of the higher-ups could make people think they do, though."

"But you have dirt on them, right?"

I pause, thinking of Adams and Johnathan. Their connection to Metzler and Harris could bring trouble down on all sorts of heads. It's something I could use, but there's no telling what the consequences could be. Still, I decide to answer her truthfully.

"Yes."

Rina bites her lower lip. Her eyes have gotten brighter, showing a familiar spike in her curiosity. "Then don't just take your job back."

"What do you mean?"

"Ask for a promotion. Homicide Division or something."

"That isn't ethical, Rina."

"No? What they're doing to you is unethical, Harvey. What I'm suggesting is fair."

I consider what Rina is proposing. It would be nice to have a position in the department that pays salary instead of bounty. I've always hated killing to make a decent living, but pulling such a tactic on the chief borders on blackmail. I tend to err on the side of caution; it's gotten me this far. Rina's idea is a bold move, and a potentially dangerous one.

"You owe me for not telling me sooner," Rina insists. "You've got a chance to be safer. Take it."

I fear the consequences of my decision, but I realize how right she is. *It just might work.* "OK, you're right, Rina."

"Damn straight I'm right! They have to give you something for your trouble," she says with a small but satisfied smile.

Quite proud of her cleverness, we finish our cake and go back to lighter conversation. I'm relieved that she knows that I intend to return to work. It felt wrong to keep up the charade. Her idea makes me seriously nervous, though there's a hint of excitement to the prospect. Tomorrow I'll go see Anderson. A brighter future seems closer than I've ever dreamed it could be.

CHAPTER 5

HOMICIDE DIVISION

After I see Rina off to school, I walk back home from the Fastrack to collect my things so I can head to work. The city seems unnaturally calm today. With the fresh, cool morning air on my face, I appreciate the irony: The day has taken on my typical temperament just as I'm about to succumb to the chaotic murkiness that usually personifies Motor City. My nerves are going wild, and the disturbingly sweet-scented breeze is tainted by the pungent smell of garlic emanating from my sweat glands. I can face a loaded gun with no fear, but a simple meeting with Chief Anderson has stirred up my mind and emotions.

Weakling!

It's hard to ignore the city's cruel, hissing whisper. I attempt to distract myself from her venomous speech with minutia. I think of how I modified a new gun while I was healing. My old one is rusting in an evidence bag somewhere. It felt strange to load the bullets into the clean chambers. I had to brush dust off of my old holster when I was getting ready this morning.

I fire up the hearse and make my way to the department. The route feels almost unfamiliar. The pedestrians I drive past all seem to be staring at me. I wonder if people have always watched me like this. Maybe I got used to ignoring it; I must have. I've been off duty long enough to be out of touch with the streets.

There's no parking out front, so I go down the alley and find a spot for the hearse. It's a tight fit. As I walk toward the building, I think of the brief blip about me in the news right after I woke up in the hospital. The heroic Serenity cop who survived the roughest drug bust in recent history. My sixty seconds of fame, over in a flash. Since then, the city has all but forgotten the loss of nine of her officers and the one who got away.

I didn't get away, though. I'm back again, giving Motor City another shot at me. The familiar beep of the ID scanner as I pass through the front doors might as well be the click of a trigger being cocked. The department looks exactly as it did before I left; it's been unfazed by my absence. I suddenly feel like toilet paper as I realize how disposable I truly am. Had I died in the explosion or later on the operating table, Motor City would've simply carried on without me. Feeling microscopic, I sulk over to an elevator on my right.

Once I'm in the elevator, a second ID scanner processes my bar code, and the light on the floor screen changes to green. I lightly press the button for the top floor, hoping it won't register my touch. Sadly, it does. Unlike the department's lower floors, marred by the constant flow of hundreds of officers, the top floor is almost immaculate and nearly vacant. This part of the building is one of the most recent additions, and the furnishings are clean and modern, colored in deep tones and made from expensive materials. It's a posh showcase of the department's power.

I shuffle over to a large desk in an alcove near the elevator. An automated assistant sits behind it. Eerily lifelike with its clean plastic skin and soft features, it greets me in a pleasant tone. "How can I assist you, sir?" Its voice is plain, with no gender specificity.

Its form lacks definition so that it cannot offend anyone it interacts with.

"I have a meeting with Chief Mark Anderson."

A quick scan of the bar code on my head is enough for the assistant to recognize me. "Yes, Officer Havoc, Serenity Division, Chief Anderson is expecting you. Down the hall and the first door on your left, sir."

"Thanks."

"You are welcome, sir."

I head down the hall to Anderson's office. As with the rest of the fixtures on this level, the door to the office is ornate. It's classical in design, made of richly colored hardwood, with a brass knob. The fingerprint identification pad and ID scanner to access the room, however, break up the natural flow.

Inside, I find Anderson seated behind a smart desk larger than any I've seen before. As the door closes, he greets me. "Nice to see you again, Harvey. Please have a seat."

The furnishings in his office are twentieth-century modern. Anderson is clearly a man of taste. I seat myself in the stylish chair he is gesturing toward, which positions me directly across from him.

"I see from Dr. Arnold's report that you have a clean bill of health," he says.

"Yes, back to normal, sir."

"Good. How is your sister?"

"Good. It was nice to have some time off; gave us a chance to catch up on things."

"I'm glad to hear it, Harvey." *So we're on a first-name basis. Interesting.* "I haven't noticed you submit a letter of retirement."

The nerves are welling up in me. I fear that Anderson will read the discomfort on my face or notice that I'm sweating. "I haven't, sir."

"Are you still considering it, Harvey?"

My heart's pounding so fast that he may hear it from across the desk. I swallow hard and force the words out. "That depends, sir."

Anderson leans back in his chair, his jaw clenching slightly. "On what, Harvey?"

"I don't enjoy having to make quota to survive, sir. I would prefer a position that pays salary."

"Is that so? Like a place in the Homicide Division, perhaps?"

"Yes, sir."

He shakes his head, looking half annoyed, half admiring. "I have to admit, Harvey, you have bigger balls than half the men in this department to ask me a question like that."

"You said you want me to stay on instead of retiring. This way, we both get what we want out of a bad situation."

"You wouldn't be trying to stack the deck in your favor, Harvey, would you?" he asks in a voice that could cut glass.

Shit. I resist the urge to shift in my seat. "No, sir. Just asking for something I believe I deserve."

Anderson chews on my words for a minute before he replies. "OK, Havoc. Have it your way."

He's switched back to calling me Havoc. Our relationship has ceased being friendly and returned to pure professionalism. The chief turns on the large screen of his smart desk and begins to type as the desktop angles toward him. I wait with my hands folded in my lap and my back straight.

"It's done, Havoc," he says brusquely after a few minutes. "I've sent you some information to review before you report in on Monday."

An unnerving mixture of relief and trepidation fills me. I let out a meek "Thank you, sir."

He shakes his head. "Before you thank me, let me get two things completely straight with you. First, the topic of the bust as conversation ends right now. Second, I expect the best from any detective I appoint to the Homicide Division. This is not a gift, Havoc. If I don't see results from you in your new position, I will waste no time in demoting you back to Serenity. If you screw up badly enough, I will send you all the way back to Street Division. Are we clear?"

"Yes, sir. Crystal clear."

"Good. You will report to the Homicide Division on Monday at eight."

"Yes, sir."

I stand up and hold out my hand to Anderson. He rises and shakes it firmly. We make eye contact. "Good luck, Havoc," he says.

Leaving the station, I again get the sense that everyone's eyes are on me. It's as if they know what I've done. This strange unrest stays with me as I drive through the busy Friday morning streets of Motor City. By the time I get home, the feeling has dissipated somewhat, and my remaining unease is directed at the speed with which Anderson agreed to my request. *There must be some kind of catch to his deal,* I decide, but this thought pales in comparison to the realization of what I have just become. Success in the Homicide Division will mean I no longer need to maintain a body count to make an income. Perhaps I'm not as small in my own world as I previously felt.

I make myself a cup of coffee and sit down at the kitchen table to start reviewing the information Anderson has sent. I put my transponder in read-aloud mode and listen to its methodical voice spell out everything I need to know about detective work and the Homicide Division. Much of the information covered is familiar; I spent a year studying homicide investigation in school. In the past, I would've had to have on-the-job training before being considered for a detective position in Homicide. These days, if you survive Motor City as an officer as long as I have, the time served in any position is experience enough. Still, some of the information is new to me, and I pay close attention to the material I don't recognize.

After a few dry hours of this, I shut off the transponder to take a break. Though the house is quiet again, the city outside bustles louder than ever. I find myself thinking of a time before I became a government-sanctioned killer, long before there was a tattoo on the side of my head to make me stand out in a crowd. I lean back in the chair and close my eyes, hoping for a brief rest, and allow my thoughts to drift back.

The world was so different when Rina and I were kids. There was no mandatory service, no blatant killing of criminals and disregard for human life. Our parents were kind, hardworking people. They took the risk of moving to Motor City for good jobs in the emerging vehicle remanufacturing industry that was bringing the city back to her feet again. My father opened a small repair shop with a few local employees, mostly young people straight out of the foster system. My mother took care of the books and got her hands dirty when my dad was short-staffed. Our parents taught us to be safe, logical, and kind. My earliest memories are some of the fondest to look back on.

The world was as it had been for as long as anyone could remember; the trouble was how many people were being born into it. Just after the turn of the last century, there was no contract killing on this scale. Despite the fact that countries and the people in them were constantly at each other's throats, no one could have dreamed it would come to this.

I remember seeing some guy on the street shoot a young woman in front of Rina and me when I was only fifteen. Looking back on it now, I think he may have been on Tech. I'll never forget the distant, haunted look in his eyes. Rina screamed, and I grabbed onto her as tight as I could and we ran for home. When we finally made it, I told my mother and father what had happened as Rina continued to sob. I still think of what my father told me, usually after I awaken from a nightmare: "Son, really bad people are crazy enough to ignore their humanity. Don't ignore your humanity."

Later that same week, there was a news broadcast—I can replay it in my mind as if it was yesterday—announcing that Tech was running rampant in the streets of Motor City. A few days after that, the riot broke out that changed the world and my life forever. Thousands died in one night, mostly around the Blue Orchid District, the heart of Tech territory. Some self-righteous uptown Motor City citizens had taken it upon themselves to rid our fair city of her Tech plight. The dealers and the Techies fought back. Soon half the city was trying to kill the other half, a veritable civil war.

Martial law was temporarily instated, and soon after that, the new laws on police service and crime were announced. At the time, the Serenity Act seemed, to my childish mind, a reasonable solution to a terrible problem, and other countries soon followed suit with their own versions of the act. Unfortunately, as the weeks and then months passed, its imperfections began to show. Outrage over the audacious plans of politicians and leaders sparked a wildfire in the people of our world, and hundreds of thousands died in the ongoing riots. Vigilantism became more aggressive, and Techies became more desperate. Walking the streets of Motor City became dangerous for anyone, including—fatally, one night—our parents.

To Rina and me, the loss of our parents was horrific; to the rest of the world, they were just two more bodies among thousands in Motor City alone. With their deaths, I came to realize that even good people can be crazy enough to accept the inhumane when they're frightened enough.

Our parents hadn't even been protesting; they were killed by some random drug-crazed Techie hell-bent on stealing money to get a fix. A couple of the newly appointed officers took us to the morgue to say goodbye. We were given only a brief moment with them, and both of us cried for hours afterward. We held each other as tight as we could, intending never to let go. Rina screamed when they separated us into foster care. She was only eleven; I was fifteen. I begged them to keep us together, but my pleas fell on deaf ears.

I thought that I might never see her again. The odds that one or both of us would die were high. But in the back of my mind, I promised myself I would find her, and that kept me going. It gave me a reason to fight. Over the next few years, the riots calmed down. The body count had only fueled the fires of the politicians' rhetoric, and the need for a new world order became paramount. The Serenity Division was the ultimate answer, and it was added to every police force across the globe.

The sudden increase in orphaned children oiled the machine of career testing. With so few unbroken homes to place children into, most older children were sent to newly created vocational homesteads. This left the state with thousands of mouths to feed, so, the thinking went, why not put that investment to good use? If every child was educated and then tested into a career, fewer of them would end up on the street. This would help lower the crime rate as well as increase the workforce in the larger cities.

I was sent to a vocational homestead outside Motor City. They didn't tell me where they sent Rina. The younger kids studied, and the older ones worked in some of the new remanufacturing plants. The Shop teacher there, Mr. Desoto, reaffirmed my father's teachings of self-reliance and humanity. I got back in touch with myself through learning about cars.

By the time I was eighteen and considered an adult, the riots were a thing of the past. The bloodstained streets in the big cities across the world had dried over and scabbed up into something new. The laws were arguably working; the population was going down day by day. In the end, the trick to calming the riots was promising that the laws were only temporary and that the Serenity Divisions could go away once the global population was reduced by 15 percent. To me, this seems like a false promise. The plan has worked far too well for the politicians to dismantle it so quickly.

By the time I turned twenty-one, the population was down by 8 percent. I remember the statistic well, because it was that same year that I found Rina. I was barely old enough to be accepted as her legal guardian. We got a small apartment, and educational grants paid the rent. The first couple of years with Rina back in my life were rough. She had a hard time in the foster system, worse than anything I had endured.

She was one of the "lucky" few to be placed in an actual home, because she was still so young, an attribute more desirable to families looking to adopt. The state hadn't done much in the way of background checks. If they had, they would've seen her foster father's abuse record. The bastard and his sniveling wife had three foster children besides my sister, and he beat all of them. After a time, he got bored with that, so he raped them. When I first found Rina, she barely recognized me. I had to fight hard to get her trust me. She had ample reason to hate and distrust men. I would have probably killed her foster father if I'd had the chance, but he skipped town.

Somehow, we got through the worst of it. I wish I could say I was able to inspire Rina's faith in humanity to come back, but the truth is less romantic. It took years of therapy and her hating my rules before she turned around. Even then, it was years more till we truly saw eye to eye. Eventually, she made some good friends at school and found a few teachers who believed in her. They ended up helping her make the turnaround I couldn't provide on my own.

At twenty-five, I tested for career placement. My scores were, disappointingly, a perfect match for an officer of the law. We both cried when I told Rina the news. We thought I'd die in the first few months. Somehow I didn't; somehow I've gotten this far. The population is holding at 13.5 percent down, so our world is close to the proposed end of this madness. And as of this morning, I will no longer be forced to kill to survive.

"How did it go?"

I almost fall out of the chair on hearing Rina's voice and the sound of her books hitting the table with a thud. I must've dozed off. From the corner of my eye, I can see the light dimming to a cool blue outside the kitchen window.

"Well, your idea worked," I say, allowing a yawn to escape.

"Really?"

"Yep. You are looking at Detective Harvey Havoc, Homicide Division."

"Wow. No longer a glorified hitman!"

"Nope. Just the salaried detective life for me."

Rina rushes over and hugs me tight enough to make my lungs ache. "Thank God, or whomsoever is watching. I was getting tired of worrying about you."

"Well, it's still a dangerous job, sis."

"True, but statistically, detectives live longer than all other officers in the MCPD," Rina points out.

"True," I echo.

"When do you start?" she asks, sounding almost giddy.

"Monday."

Rina raises a curious eyebrow. "Have you studied yet?"

"A bit," I reply, wary of information overload.

"Want some help?"

"Sure."

While I cook dinner, Rina uses my transponder to ask me questions. It's nice to feel like I'm heading toward something better. This feeling is warm and embracing compared to the way I felt this morning. *Maybe in two years' time, the population will be down to an acceptable level, and maybe Rina won't have to test,* I think. *Perhaps the scheming politicians will live up to their word. Wouldn't that be something?*

If there's anything that I could give to save Rina from being trapped in my line of work, I would do it in a heartbeat. She's too smart for it. She doesn't deserve to see the horrible things

I've seen. I don't want her to become a killer like I am, on the razor's edge of humanity. I don't want her to have to cheat death just to get a chance at something better for her future.

We study on and off over the rest of the weekend, watching the *Back to the Future* trilogy in between. I clean up around the house a little more, trying to make my transition back to full-time work easier. We take a walk to the Fastrack and go to the City Meadows park for a few hours on Sunday afternoon to see a performance by Punk Band X. The late summer air is almost sweet smelling, carried in by a gentle breeze from across the nearby water. It's a far cry from the usual smog. The music isn't quite my jam; I prefer vintage rock from the early 2000s. It makes Rina happy, though, and that's enough reason for me to enjoy it.

Everyone's wild haircuts and in-your-face clothing make me feel like I'm immersed in '90s punk culture. The sizable turnout puts my senses on high alert initially, but once I start to pay attention to the crowd, I see how happy they are. This isn't like watching "normal" people on the street in their slick, modern-looking, bland-hued outfits, and I can't remember when I saw so many people in one place having fun for fun's sake. For me, the concert is a window into the lighter side of Motor City. It's refreshing to know that my world isn't filled with only two-dimensional people. It's also nice to have an event where no one dies; that never seems to happen for me. I'm glad that Rina convinced me to wear a hat to cover my tattoo. If she hadn't, I don't think the crowd would have been as welcoming.

The band rocks hard and plays an extra set, and the crowd goes wild for the special treat. The charismatic lead singer, Crimson Xenos, jumps into the elated crowd at the end, and they carry him aloft as if he is a god. As we leave, I decide that this has been one of the most carefree experiences of my life, a perfect way to spend my time before starting my new job. But as Sunday night rolls in, I find myself unable to sit still. I wonder if detective work will be better or worse than Serenity Division. If I fail at it, Anderson will cut me down to a Street officer in an instant. I cannot let that happen. I have to make the most of this chance at something new. As I fall asleep, I resolve that I'll succeed. This is my shot in the dark, and I'm taking it for my own good and for Rina's future. I will be the best detective that the MCPD has ever seen, because I want it; I need it.

The next morning comes into glaring clarity with the obnoxious alarm on my transponder. The ringing in my ears is enough to make my mood decidedly different than last night's optimism. A glance at the time in the corner of the transponder screen reveals that it's almost eight. I've snoozed the alarm three times too many.

I hastily put on a nice tie and white button-up shirt with black jeans. I decide to keep wearing my steel-toed boots despite their informal look. I finish off my outfit with a slick leather jacket I bought a few years ago for nice occasions.

When I make it to the kitchen, I see that Rina is ready to leave. She rolls her eyes at me for being late on my first day and gives me a one-armed hug before heading to the Fastrack station. I notice that she has earbuds in, which explains why she didn't know I hadn't gotten up. She's probably listening to PBX, which would definitely be too loud for her to hear my alarm. I gulp down some instant breakfast and make sure I have all of my gear packed in the hearse. I also double check my new gun and ensure that I have plenty of ammo.

The traffic is heavy, and I lose more time than I hoped to on my way to work. The Homicide Division is in the newer part of the MCPD. There also happens to be parking in the main garage reserved for all detectives. I'm pleased with this perk, and with a little luck, it'll make for a faster route into the building.

An automated parking assistant at the gate scans my plate number and the bar code on the side of my head to assign me a place. This assistant looks more machinelike than human and is more robust than the ones inside, no doubt to deal with the odd sideswipe from a passing car. A bullet mark on the side of its bulky, all-metal figure indicates that at least one officer has become angry with it. It downloads a map of the garage to the screen on my dash. I follow the directions to a spot on the second story. The LED sign on the wall above it reads "DETECTIVE HAVOC." It's a tight fit, so I decide to back the hearse in.

By the time I take the elevator to the Homicide Division, my transponder is reading 8:05. This is definitely not the way to become the best detective in Motor City. At this rate, I'll be lucky to last a week. Inside, I see another automated assistant to pick up my badge. This assistant is the same inoffensive, nondescript model as the one outside Anderson's office. After searching through a small drawer in its desk, it hands me an ornate gold-plated badge. Perhaps the most vintage-looking things in the whole building, the badges are a tradition held over from the early twentieth century.

I go through a set of double doors under a large sign that reads "HOMICIDE DIVISION." A bar code reader scans my tattoo as I enter. My heart sinks. The room is largely deserted. An old clock on the wall at the far end of the room reads 8:15. I've missed the meeting for morning assignments.

On the other side of the room, one remaining detective is seated behind a smart desk. He looks to be in his midforties, with freckles dotting skin the color of strong coffee. He has on a pair of glasses, an odd choice given today's readily available corrective surgery options. Officers' health care is considered second to none, including dental and eye care. His must be a choice of tradition rather than convenience. I would guess that this is case with Sergeant Mitchell as well; she's the only other person I know who wears glasses.

He doesn't look in my direction. Even when I hover over his desk, he continues to type without acknowledging me. I clear my throat, but he doesn't bother to look up.

"You Havoc?" he asks dismissively.

"Yes, sir."

"It's 8:15. Morning assignments are given out at eight on a Monday."

"Sorry, sir. It won't happen again."

He takes off his glasses and puts them in a drawer of the smart desk, then shuts off the screen. Looking at me for the first time, he speaks curtly. "There's really no reason for you to call me 'sir.' My name's Walter Evans; most call me Walt."

"Sorry, Walt, won't happen again."

"I hope not. That is, of course, not if you plan on being lead detective for long, anyways."

My jaw drops at his words. Walt stands up, revealing that he's taller than I am by a few inches. He's wearing well-fitted slacks and a dark blue button-up shirt with a checkered tie. He smirks as he says, "Let me guess, no one bothered to tell you it's a lead detective position."

"Shit, no." *What the hell is going on?*

"Great," Walt says, shaking his head.

"Shouldn't lead go to someone more experienced than me?"

"Yeah, I can think of a couple detectives in this department that're going to be pissed to see you, Havoc."

"I didn't ask to be lead." I try not to wince as I hear how defensive I sound.

"When the chief does a favor, there's always a catch. Clever bastard is probably trying to set you up for a fast fail."

"Perfect," I sigh, deflated.

"Don't worry about it. We've all been there, kid. I sent you the info on your case just now. Your partner Smith's likely there already."

"Thanks."

"Don't mention it, kid. First day on the job always sucks." Walt winks.

I make my way back to the garage as quickly as I can and download the information Walt has sent me into the Cadillac's dash screen. I flip on my concealed lights and siren to clear a path to the location. Darting in and out of traffic wildly, I thread through narrow spaces in the hulking Cadillac, leaving only inches of clearance to spare. Within a few minutes, I am almost at the crime scene. Hopefully, things will start to go better from here.

I'm getting tired of this shit.

CHAPTER 6

DETECTIVE SMITH

I pull into an available space across the street. There's a morgue van and several cop cars present, as well as a boxy old CSI van with a dented-in front fender. The officers are congregating in the alley between two of the large apartment buildings that dominate this neighborhood. This isn't a half bad part of town, really. Rina and I looked at a place here a few years back, but it was far out of our price range.

An officer with his shirt half untucked comes running across the street, waving his arms excitedly. I roll down the window as he skids on his heels to an abrupt stop. He has likely recognized the hearse, and he confirms my identity with a glance at the tattoo on the side of my head.

"Ah, Havoc. Smith's been waiting for you," he says.

"Really? That wasn't necessary," I reply, not sure why Smith would wait for me. It's my fault this show is on hold.

I get out and follow the unkempt, young-looking officer across the street. There are several crime scene investigators taking notes and inspecting the alley. The other cops are talking among themselves. Occasionally they stop to ward a civilian away. The cool morning air is starting to give way to the typical Motor City smog. Some sunlight is breaking through the clouds, casting long shadows from the vast brick and mortar apartments. As I duck under the police tape, I put on a pair of latex gloves.

The alley is long and narrow. Approximately ten feet wide, it ends in a wall about a hundred feet ahead. There's only one door opening onto it, at the end and to the right. There are a few sad-looking little windows that overlook the alley. The glass in them is opaque. Even if someone watched this murder from above, they'd be able to tell us little of worth. There's a row of rusted green and brown dumpsters near the back wall on the left side of the alley. The bare foot of a corpse is sticking out from the small space between the last dumpster and the wall.

As I start down the alley, I cannot help but be distracted by a striking-looking woman leaning against the wall to my left. She's tall and slender, her hair short and electric blue. A vibrant contrast to her light skin, it stands up in chaos and makes the deep blue of her eyes smolder like the pilot flame on a gas stovetop. I think back to Tek's comment about tattoos affecting genetics due to Tech use. I wonder if this woman's hair is naturally such an intense color If so, it's either because of Tech or she's from another planet.

She's smoking a cigarette, something I haven't known anyone to do in a long time. Her dark, fitted blue jeans have a hole in the right knee, and her white T-shirt has some sort of logo on it that I can't quite make out, as it's partially obscured by a well-worn gray leather jacket. As I pass her, I note that her thick-heeled boots bring her to near my own height. Interestingly, her eyebrows match her hair. *The blue must be natural*, I think, *though I guess she could just as easily have a dedicated hair stylist on Venus.*

I'm glad to have a witness, but it would be even better to know who my partner is. I consider investigating the body by myself, but I decide it would be in poor taste to both keep Smith waiting and then start without him. I turn back to ask after him.

I walk past the striking woman again, the left side of her face in the shadow of the buildings that loom over us on either side. She's taking a long drag on her cigarette. I go back to where the group of cops can easily hear me.

"Is Smith here yet?" I call out. My question is met with laughter and head shaking among the other officers. I'm answered from behind.

"I got here ten minutes ago, dumbass."

Her voice is smooth despite its high pitch. She's clearly irritated. I turn to see her putting out the cigarette on the wall beside her. She's careful to dispose of it in a small tin she has taken from her jacket pocket, no doubt in an effort to avoid contaminating the scene. She looks me up and down as she moves away from the wall. Now that she's facing me, I can see that the left side of her head is cleanly shaved to expose her bar code tattoo.

"So, you're Anderson's idea of a lead detective. Freaking fantastic. I get the Wanna-Be Reaper," Smith says, shaking her head slightly.

I hold out my hand for her to shake, unsure what else to do. "I'm Harvey."

"Harvey Havoc. Cute."

She ignores my hand and takes a sucker out of her jacket to replace the cigarette. She puts on a pair of latex gloves, then turns her back on me and walks down the alley toward the body. I hear more chuckling from behind me as I follow her. She walks tall, with purpose in each step. I hang my shoulders as I trail behind her. It was careless of me to assume Smith was a man.

There's no particular odor of decay besides the one from the dumpsters themselves, which leads me to think the body is relatively fresh. Smith crouches down beside it in the narrow space between the dumpster and the wall. She's careful to ensure that she doesn't tread on any evidence: I watch my step too. The blanket over the victim looks fairly expensive. There's quite a bit of blood on it and on the pavement around the body. Smith pulls the blanket gently back.

The body of the woman underneath is a mess. Her face is bruised and beaten, her blonde hair reddened with blood. There are several stab wounds to her chest. The closeness of the wounds makes it difficult to tell how many. Like the blanket, the dress she's wearing looks expensive. She appears to have been in her early twenties, and in life, she would have ticked all the boxes for society's definition of beauty.

"Well, what do you make of her, Detective Havoc?" Smith says this with a mocking tone, though her eyes make it clear she's poking fun at me and not the situation at hand.

I consider the scene, then say, "The blanket and clothes are expensive; so's the jewelry. I'd say she hasn't been here long, maybe since early this morning. Her jewelry and purse are still here, so I'd assume that rules out robbery."

Smith carefully lifts the woman's skirt. We both look only long enough to see that she still has her panties on.

"Well, that rules out sexual motive." Smith sounds definite.

"Just because she still has her underwear on? He could've put them back on after."

Smith rolls the sucker to the other side of her mouth before replying. "Yeah? Our killer could've been a she, too."

Ouch. "OK, Smith, you're right. I'm an idiot. A sexist idiot. Just tell me what happened and I can get out of your way."

"It's not just about the panties," Smith says, exasperated. "Also, her body was covered, and she was stabbed repeatedly. What does that say to you when you put it all together?"

"Whoever did this was angry enough to stab her, but stabbing is a pretty intimate way to kill someone, and they cared enough to cover her up and leave her personal things. It's almost like they were sorry."

Smith eyes me with feigned admiration. "Well, shit, Havoc, you're not just a wanna-be after all. Might be hope for you yet."

"A rapist wouldn't try to tidy up afterward. They wouldn't care for her dignity," I continue, ignoring her snide remarks.

"Exactly."

"Why here, though?"

"That's the real question, Havoc. Why here?"

Smith straightens up and motions for one of the CSIs to come over and log the evidence. She then calls over one of the other officers. "I want you to go check in with both building managers," she instructs him. "I need to know who has access to the door here in the alley."

The officer nods in response to her command and goes off on his assignment. Smith turns to inspect the door. She presses down on the handle a few times. The biometric ID screen on the wall next to the door remains black. Either it's out of service or can only be activated from within.

"I bet her fingerprint can unlock this door," Smith says.

I nod in agreement.

"Probably lives in one of these apartments."

Her words are firm, but I risk testing her logic. "Maybe. Or she could've been seeing someone here."

Without bothering to reply, Smith begins to search the alley. After a time, I decide to inquire, "What're you looking for?"

"A murder weapon would be handy. You need evidence to catch a killer. If you really want to be a detective, you might consider joining me."

I let this slide and quietly help her look. There's an overabundance of information here that appears to have nothing to do with this woman's death. Dumpsters full of trash. Walls painted with colorful graffiti from local gangs and street artists. Cockroaches living on a veritable smorgasbord of refuse. Even on this minute scale, Motor City is voraciously consuming herself.

After several silent minutes of searching, I'm relieved to be the one to find a knife wedged under one of the dumpsters. Maybe this will change Smith's attitude toward me. I point it out to the CSI who is taking detailed photos of the body.

"This makes things easier," I say.

"Not much," Smith replies, holding up her own discovery.

I walk over to see what she's referring to. My ego is quickly squashed. Smith has found a set of bloodied gloves in one of the other dumpsters.

"Great. So we're still nowhere," I say.

"Everything has a meaning, Havoc. Now we know that our killer's careful."

"So we have a careful murderer with regret for what they've done."

"Yeah, nice narrow suspect pool, isn't it?" Smith says, a small smirk playing across her lips.

"Yeah, a real win."

"Let's hand this over to the CSIs. We should have a chat with the building manager ourselves."

Smith leaves the alley, and I follow her like a lost puppy. I'm not sure how well this lead detective thing is going to work. Half an hour in, and I'm doing a piss-poor job of observing my surroundings; not only that, but my partner already hates me. I'm barely leading myself, let alone a department.

We dispose of our gloves by bagging them and hand them off to one of the CSIs. He labels each bag carefully, then adds it to an ever-growing pile that will later be processed. Smith and I head into the lobby of the apartments to the right of the alley. We tell the automated assistant behind the concierge desk that we need to see the manager, and it directs us to the elevators. It's hardly a surprise to find that his apartment's on the top floor; managers always seem to get the best rooms. The silence between Smith and me during our ride up is more than a little awkward. I can tell she would prefer to be doing all of this on her own.

Halfway to the top floor, I decide to make another attempt at conversation.

"How long have you been a detective in the Homicide Division?" I ask her.

"Two years this week," she says curtly.

"Impressive. You must be gifted to have been in it for so much of your service."

"Would've been even more impressive if I had made lead detective. Looks before experience, I guess."

My heart sinks. "Shit. Anderson gave me your job, didn't he?"

"Yep."

"Sorry."

"Apologies are for wanna-bes, Havoc. When you give up, I'll be there to step in."

I wish I'd kept silent. *At least now I know why she doesn't like me.* The elevator makes it to the top floor, and we exit into a long hall. The manager's apartment is on the end. We walk in silence toward the door. Just before we reach it, Smith removes the bare sucker stick from between her lips and flicks it expertly into a nearby trash can. I knock on the door.

A man's face appears on the screen by the doorframe. "How can I help you?" he asks.

Smith speaks up first. "I'm Detective Smith. This is my partner, Detective Havoc. Can we have a word?"

"Got ID?" the man asks.

Smith pulls out her badge. I fumble to retrieve mine. After the man carefully examines our badges, he buzzes the door open.

Maybe six inches shorter than Smith, he's heavyset, with a graying beard, and balding. He beckons us into a well-furnished sitting room. Smith and I sit in some stylish chairs across from the large couch that he seats himself on.

"How can I help?" His tone is calm, yet inquisitive.

Smith seems distracted, her eyes scanning the apartment. I can't help but wonder what she's looking for. I decide to take the initiative with the manager. "We're interested in anything you might know about this woman." I bring up a picture of the body on my transponder. "I warn you, it isn't pleasant."

He nods, and I turn the screen to face him. "Oh my God!" he gasps. "That's May Alistair. She moved in a few months back— August, I think."

"Are you sure it's her?"

"Fairly sure. Hard to forget a form like hers. Such a shame. This city is always brimming with senseless violence. When will it stop?"

Unfazed by his woeful statement, Smith abruptly checks back into the conversation. "What apartment did she rent?"

"Five twenty-three. Fifth floor, obviously."

"Thanks," Smith says. Then she's out of her chair and heading for the door. The manager, who hasn't even had a chance to introduce himself, looks shocked and confused.

"Thanks for your time, sir. We'll let you know if we have any more questions." After my hasty words, I get up and follow Smith. She's headed for the elevator with purpose.

"What the hell was that, Smith? We hardly asked him anything."

She presses the elevator button before answering me. "You really should be paying more attention to your surroundings, Havoc."

"How is this my fault?" I raise my hands from my sides in protest.

"Did you see the artwork in his apartment? Mostly male nudes. The whole place was full of fine furnishings. There was a framed photo of him and another man when they were young, and judging by their body language, they had a close relationship. He only has a bit of gray showing, even though he's clearly old enough to be all gray, and there was a large rainbow flag magnet on his fridge. Not to mention, he referred to her 'form' instead of calling her attractive. What do you think that all adds up to, Havoc?"

"He's gay?" I ask, bewildered.

"Definitely. And we're looking for a suspect who'd get mad enough at a woman to stab her several times. They'd have to love someone to get that angry, or at least think they loved them. I mean, even you must know that most murdered women are killed by a current or former romantic partner."

"Right," I sigh, outclassed again.

The elevator arrives, and we get in. I press the button for the fifth floor. I'm thankful that this elevator ride is shorter than the last one. There's little point in more attempts at pleasant conversation. Once we get out on the fifth floor, we walk side by side to May's apartment. Smith uses a combination of her badge and a scan of her bar code tattoo to override the lock. We both put on another set of gloves, then Smith slips a set of shoe covers over her boots. I realize I've forgotten to bring my own. She notices my guilty expression and retrieves an extra set for me while rolling her eyes.

Once inside, we discover that all of the lights are off, which I find odd. "Why would she turn out all of the lights if she was leaving to meet someone in the alley in the dark?"

"Yeah. That's strange." Smith's tone is almost dismissive. "Lights on," she calls out.

Nothing happens.

I echo Smith's command. "Lights on."

Still nothing.

"Now that's even more strange," Smith muses. "If her lighting is voice sensitive, it would've had to have been her who shut the lights off."

She has a point, but there's another possible explanation. "Yeah. Unless she had someone else's voice programmed into her system besides hers."

Smith turns and looks me in the eye. Though it's dark, I can see that small smirk play across her lips again. "Now that's thinking like a detective. Keep that up and I may have to fight for your job yet."

She goes to the control panel by the door and sets about investigating the lighting controls. After a while, she provides an update. "It shows that there were multiple voices enabled for the lighting. May's is the only one identified."

"Can we access the other voice patterns?"

"No, we're locked out. We'll have to put someone from the Technical Division on it later."

She messes with the access screen for a while longer before the lights come on throughout the apartment. It's well furnished, every item in its place, and too clean for any part of May's ordeal to have occurred here. Like her clothing, everything in her apartment looks expensive. I could work the rest of my days in the department and never be able to afford half of the things here.

"Maybe somebody killed her to get this apartment."

Though I mean it as a joke, Smith nods in agreement. "Yeah. No shit."

Smith and I split up to search the rooms. I take the bedroom and bath, while Smith goes over the kitchen and living room. As with the alley below, there's quite a bit to look at, but little of significance. I find no out-of-place items, nor any clothing that appears to belong to someone besides May.

There are a few sex toys and some expensive bras and panties in the bottom drawer of her dresser, the panties neatly folded and the toys carefully cleaned. It's one of the most organized bedrooms I have ever seen. I find it strange that there are no pictures of family or friends around the apartment. Only a few pieces of fine art adorn the richly dark red walls in her bedroom.

Smith and I meet back up in the living room. She has a look of disappointment on her face that must be comparable to my own. "Anything?"

"Some sex toys and expensive underwear. A taste for bold paint colors." I shrug. "You see anything?"

"Nope. Expensive wine. Fridge is full of health food crap."

"Great, so we still have nothing useful."

"Yeah. No pictures of anyone in the house, either," Smith says, her voice shaky for the first time. I wonder about that.

"I noticed that too. It's almost like this isn't her real home or something."

"We should do some more background checks on her at the station. It could be we're looking at a high-end call girl here," Smith says, leaning against a lavish brown sofa.

"It's a big risk to do that kind of thing inside the city limits these days. The fines are outrageous," I reply.

"Yeah, and the sex workers are usually the ones who get stuck with them, not their clients. But men tend to be given the advantage over women, no matter how wrong it is. Or unfair."

Her words are another obvious jab at me for being promoted over her. I choose not to retort. We leave the lights on and lock up on our way out after placing our gloves and shoe covers in plastic bags to hand off to the CSIs. They'll be up to do a sweep of the room once they're done in the alley. Back in the elevator, I decide to risk small talk again.

"You haven't told me your first name yet."

"It's tattooed on the side of my head. Can't you read?" Smith asks in an increasingly familiar irritated tone.

"I thought it was more polite to ask."

Smith rolls her eyes and turns her head so I can read the name above her bar code tattoo. I also notice that the logo on her shirt is a Cadillac badge. Her hands are in her jacket pockets, holding it open just enough so I can make out the image.

"Shay, that's an interesting name."

"Sure, whatever. Just call me Smith, all right, Havoc?"

I give up on the small talk as the elevator makes its way down. I follow Smith across the lobby and onto the street outside the apartment building's double doors. The officers have blocked off part of the sidewalk now in addition to the alley, and a few of them come over for information on May's apartment. Smith tells them the floor and number, and they brush past us to go get a closer look. We hand off our bagged gloves and shoe covers to the CSIs as they head up after the officers.

Smith takes out a fresh cigarette and lights it. As she takes the first long drag from it, she gazes off into the distance. For a time, neither of us says anything; we just stand there awkwardly in thought. Traffic passes and pedestrians go by, unconcerned by the scene in the alley. *Motor City doesn't give a shit about May, but I do. She deserves justice just as much as anyone.*

I decide to speak up first. "What do you want to look into next?"

Smith takes a few more drags before answering me. "You see those street cameras?"

I scan the street and notice two cameras. "Yeah. I see them."

"We should go back to the department and check the footage in the area, see if there's anything out of place."

"Sounds good to me."

We continue to stand there as Smith finishes her cigarette, but even when she's almost done with it, she doesn't move, her feet firmly planted as if she has no place to go.

I get tired of the silence. "You have a car?"

"Yep."

"So you don't need a ride back to the station?"

"The starter's fucked up. Got to take it to a shop. Haven't gotten to it yet."

"How'd you get here?"

"I caught a ride from one of the other detectives who's working another crime in the area."

"You want a ride with me, then?"

"I guess, if you're offering it."

With these unenthusiastic words, she drops the cigarette and grinds it out with her boot. I walk across the street, Smith close behind me. She doesn't seem to be fazed by the hearse. I suppose her shirt indicates that she's as into Cadillacs as I am. When she slides into the seat, Elli's scanner goes crazy. But oddly, just as I'm raising my hand to rap the side of the screen, the scanner decides to accept Smith on its own. *Strange. Elli always seems to have a hard time accepting new IDs. Why wouldn't she act up now?* I shrug it off and authorize Smith as a passenger. I don't have to explain the seat belt to her. She must drive a vehicle at least a few decades old.

I hesitate before starting the Cadillac, realizing that the last person I cleared to ride in my car was Ramirez. Reluctantly, I take a deep breath before deleting his info, then start up Elli and pull out onto the street. Smith is tense, as if being this close to me has made her backtrack on getting comfortable with me. I don't see a way to please her. She'll probably always find something to be annoyed with me about.

The ride back to the department is awkwardly quiet. Only the deep drone of the V8 and the hum of Motor City outside break the silence. I decide to try to cut the tension with more small talk.

"What kind of a Cadillac do you drive?"

"How do you know I drive a Cadillac?"

"I assumed, from your shirt."

Smith looks down at her shirt as if she had no idea what she was wearing until this moment. "Lucky guess. I've got a '70 Eldorado."

That pretty much ends the conversation.

When we get to the department, I pull into the garage and find my parking space, backing in as before. We head for the Technical Division, on the second story. I'm thankful that it's a brief elevator trip compared to the one in May's apartment building. These awkward silences are killing me. The automated assistant outside the door to the Tech Division politely asks us the nature of our visit. Smith downloads the information on our case from her transponder to the data scanner on the assistant's desk.

The assistant thanks us, and the door to the right of the desk unlocks and opens. There are a few dozen smart desks crammed into the medium-sized room. We're the only ones here. We seat ourselves at two desks next to each other in the far corner, then log into them and adjust the angle of the screens to fit our comfort level. We sign documents agreeing to the division's usage terms. There's irony in the fact that we're being recorded by camera as we look through the camera database. Big Brother is always watching.

It doesn't take us long to discover that there are six cameras within a short distance of our crime scene. Smith and I each take three and start reviewing footage. We decide to check everything a couple of hours before and after May's death. I realize it's going to become a long and boring first day on the job. *I guess that's better than embarrassing myself more at another crime scene.*

The next couple of hours pass by with nothing gained. Around 12:30, I take a break and go get us some lunch from the cafeteria. Not knowing what Smith might want, I grab some simple ham and cheese sandwiches and a couple of bags of chips, and I get us each a cup of coffee with cream and sugar to wash down the plain meal.

I find Smith in the same blank staredown with the screen as when I left. Her elbow is on the edge of the desk, and she's propping up her head with her palm. I put the sandwich and chips down, the coffee beside them. She mumbles a distracted "Thanks" and starts eating the sandwich without letting her eyes leave the screen.

Unlike Smith, I choose not to view footage as I eat. After I enjoy my food for a while, I force myself back to the boring task at hand. There was a brief time in which the department used a software system for this kind of thing. Unfortunately, it proved to be too inaccurate compared to the trained eye. If you want something done right in this world, you have to do it yourself.

By around three in the afternoon, Smith has fallen asleep in her chair, slumped over the smart desk with her head on her crossed arms. I pause the camera feed in front of her, deciding she could use the break. I continue to review the footage in front of me. I'm on the last of my three cameras. At around four, I too am beginning to doze in and out. The footage I'm looking at is a view of the sidewalk a few yards away from the alley. There's a sickly looking tree sprouting from a planter in the sidewalk and a small flag on a pole in front of a bakery. Only the lower half of the red flag is visible, in the upper left corner of the frame. When I first see it in my peripheral vision, I almost think I'm too tired and am imagining things.

I slap myself in the face lightly a couple of times and rewind the footage a few frames to be sure. The flag rustles in the slight breeze, no different than it has for the last few hours of footage. Then it flaps wildly in the wind for a brief moment before going back to a slow ripple.

I pause the footage and back it up to watch again. Something about the movement doesn't seem natural. Could this be what we're looking for? I nudge Smith's shoulder to wake her up. It takes her a second to realize that she dozed off. Then she glares at me and says, frustrated, "Damn it! You let me fall asleep?"

"It seemed like you could use it. Check this out, though. I think I found something."

I play back the footage for her. She looks skeptical. As the strange flag movement comes and goes, she doesn't seem to notice. I pause the footage just after that and rewind it again.

"Did you see it?" I ask.

"I think you need sleep more than I do. I didn't see anything."

"Here. Keep your eyes on the flag in the corner."

I play it back again. Smith leans over my shoulder to focus on the flag. Her eyes widen as she notices the strange movement. She brushes my hand away from the controls and rewinds it to watch one more time.

"Shit, Havoc, I think you have something here," Smith says, sounding surprised and maybe a little irritated.

I nod. "It's almost like somebody took a few seconds of footage from a windy night and looped it in to cover up something."

"Yeah, about ten seconds' worth. What time was this?" Smith asks, her eyes darting expectantly to the corner of the screen.

I pull up the time log for the footage. It reads 2:03 a.m.

"How often does this camera download?" Smith asks.

"Looks like it downloads every hour on the hour."

"Go ahead to a bit before 3 a.m." Smith says, leaning closer to the screen.

I forward the footage to 2:50 and play it. Smith and I watch intently. As I lean forward, I notice the pleasant smell of her hair. It's kind of fruity. Before, it was masked by cigarette smoke. I forget this brief distraction as I see the flag in the corner of the screen do something strange again. It goes from moving gently in the breeze to falling limp, then to waving in the breeze again.

Smith slaps the desk. "That's it, Havoc. We have our timeline."

"2:03 to 2:52 isn't much time, but it's enough if you know you're going to be killing somebody, I guess."

"More important than that, Havoc, we know we're dealing with a clever individual here. They would've had to know the camera downloads every hour and that they needed footage from another night to replace the image."

"Not to mention they would've had to break into the data storage system around the block to access this camera and change the footage before the download at 3 a.m.," I point out.

"Yep."

My mind trails back to my recent run-in with dirty cops, and an idea slips to the surface of my thoughts. I hesitate, then decide it should be said. "Do you think we're looking at a cop?"

Smith sighs deeply and stands up from her smart desk. She stretches her arms above her head as she considers my words. I turn in my chair to watch her reaction.

"That would be a real shitstorm, wouldn't it? I guess it's just as possible as anything else. We probably ought to look elsewhere first, though, before we start saying 'dirty cop,'" Smith says gravely as her eyes meet mine.

"Who else would be able to do something like this?" I wonder out loud.

"There are some amazing hackers in Motor City, Havoc. Somebody could've paid one of them to take care of the footage. You could pull some files on known hackers in the area."

"I could. Where are you going?"

Smith takes her jacket off the back of her chair and flings it over her shoulder. "It's after four, Havoc. Eight hours of you is enough for one day. I'll see you in the morning."

"Oh. Right." I pause, considering. "I might stick around and look into some hackers. We can go check a few of them out in the morning."

"Sounds fascinating. Good luck with that."

Just like that, she's gone, leaving me to do more research on my own. I save the important footage in a separate file, then stretch my arms out a bit and log into a different database for criminal records. Feeling my eyelids grow heavy, I decide to have a piece of gum to help stay awake. As I fumble around in my jacket pocket for my half-empty pack of gum, I realize that my keys are gone.

"Shit!"

I say this way louder than necessary to the empty room. I rush to close everything down and get out of the Technical Division as soon as I can. It's clear that Smith took my keys. She must've snagged them from my pocket when she leaned in to look at the footage. The question is why?

I rush through the department and wait impatiently in the elevator before making it downstairs and heading toward the garage. When I get there, I hear the labored sound of Elli's engine turning over. I'm relieved that Smith hasn't managed to get the old girl started. As I come around the corner, Smith's eyes meet mine from behind the wheel. Her expression changes from determination to disappointment, and she slumps back in the driver's seat.

I don't bother to move as fast now. I make my way purposefully over to the driver's side door of the hearse. Smith rolls her eyes at me before rolling the window down.

"Do you mind explaining what the hell you're doing with my car?" I ask through gritted teeth.

"Trying to start it." The sarcasm and defiance in her voice and eyes is incredibly frustrating.

"If you need a ride home, all you have to do is ask. You don't have to steal my fucking keys!" I yell, throwing my hands up in frustration.

"I didn't need a ride home. I was just going to borrow it for a couple hours."

"OK, so I took your job, I get it. Screw with your new partner to get even, fine. The joke's over. Either slide over or get the fuck out of my car!" I'm still yelling. I'm not sure when I was last this angry with someone.

Smith glares at me, arms crossed over her chest. After a few moments, she lets out a deep sigh and slides over the bench seat to the passenger side. I grab the handle and open the Cadillac's door so forcefully that I almost bash it into the car parked next to me. I get in and slam Elli's door harder than I meant to.

I take a deep breath. "So, where exactly were you planning on taking my car?"

"If I wanted you to know where I was going, I would've asked for a ride instead of taking your keys," she says sullenly.

"OK, look. I don't know what kind of partner you're used to having, Smith, but this is *not* how I do things. We need to trust each other. You want to borrow the car? Then ask me. You want privacy for something? I can handle that; just tell me. But you don't take my damn car with no explanation."

"Fine. You really want to go with me? Then let's go."

"Where?"

"I'll give you directions as we drive," Smith says, crossing her arms over her chest again.

I consider whether I really want her in my car anymore. I think about how much better it would be to kick her out and go home. But even if she's doing a lousy job of being a partner, I'm better than this petty bullshit. I can follow through regardless of her attitude. I start up the Cadillac.

A mechanical choke is as good of a theft deterrent as a stick shift transmission. As I pull out the choke cable to start Elli, Smith sighs deeply again.

"Who the hell puts a mechanical choke on a Cadillac?" she asks.

"Well, it stopped you, didn't it?"

The engine roars to life, and I pull out of the garage. Smith shakes her head and points to the right. I go that way. She puts on her seat belt and remains silent, providing directional input with her index finger. *She's starting to drive me crazy. She is crazy. How am I supposed to work with crazy?*

CHAPTER 7

THE OTHER SMITH

While following Smith's directions, I realize that we're heading straight for the worst part of town, the Blue Orchid District. Along the way, we drive by the hulking wreckage of the building that burned to the ground in the drug bust a few months before. I cannot help being unnerved by the sight. It's almost impossible to believe that I survived. Seeing its twisted and mangled iron skeleton rise up from piles of blackened, crushed brick, I can almost believe in miracles for the first time. *I should be dead, but somehow I've cheated death. Why me? Am I any more important than the others who died that morning?* I hold my breath until the wreckage is in the rearview mirror. Noticing my distraction, Smith finally says something.

"That was where the bust went down, wasn't it?"

"Yes."

"You must be some kind of lucky," she says with a hint of what might be envy.

I take a deep breath before responding, unsure that what happened to me was luck. "Some kind."

Smith crosses her arms and turns her gaze out of the window. I'm not sure why my words have upset her, or even if they have.

We take a few more turns and head over several blocks. I'm glad to have the burned-out building well behind me. We're farther from the water now, in an area known to be the heart of

Tech Lord territory. It's the sort of place where you don't want to stay too long at a stop sign for fear of being attacked for no other reason than existing. Smith points out a parking space, and I pull into it. There are a few other cars on the street, and all of them are expensive-looking enough to alarm me. Fancy cars in a bad neighborhood often mean only one thing. If an individual is willing to leave a car worth more than most people's homes in a place like this, that individual is not to be trifled with.

"I don't feel comfortable leaving my car here," I admit.

"Then don't. I shouldn't be too long."

With these curt words, Smith undoes her seat belt and grabs the door handle to let herself out. I put a hand on her shoulder to stop her. She glares at me, eyes ablaze. I retract my hand quickly before speaking.

"You might piss me off, but I'm not about to let my partner go out in this part of town without backup."

"Suit yourself."

She gets out, and I lock the door behind her, then get out too, careful to lock my door as well. I cross the street alongside her. As we get some distance from Elli, I look back briefly to make sure the old girl is OK. Smith notices my glance.

"Don't worry about your car," she says. "As long as it's in that spot, no one will screw with it."

I'm unsure what to make of her cryptic statement. I begrudgingly shrug it off and follow her to a large brick building on the other side of the street. It's about ten or so stories and clearly from the early twentieth century. There's a well-worn set of swinging glass doors in the archway of the entrance. I follow Smith through them.

Inside the poorly lit lobby, the air is thick with the smell of cigarette and cigar smoke. There's only one person here, a burly man behind a large counter. He appears to be in his late forties, and he has a cigar clenched between his lips. His well-tanned skin is lined with wrinkles and scars; his hair is reddish and speckled with gray. He raises a thick eyebrow when he sees us.

"Shay! Good ta see ya again, girl. How've ya been?" He has a deep voice and a thick Irish accent.

"I'm fine, Murray."

"Who's the feckin' suit?" His dark green eyes look me up and down judgmentally.

"This is my new partner, Havoc."

"Trustworthy?" he asks, leaning toward Smith and looking her in the eye.

"More so than I am," she says, grinning.

Murray chuckles at this, his smile revealing yellowed teeth.

"Is he in?" Smith asks.

"That he is. I'm sure he'll be glad ta see ya." Murray waves a hand toward a well-worn bank of elevators.

"Go ahead and buzz us up, then, Murray," Smith says.

Murray nods and presses a button under the counter. As he does, his jacket shifts, revealing a sidearm. I hear an old elevator door creak its way open on the other side of the lobby. I follow Smith into the elevator, and the door closes loudly behind us. I'm surprised when she's the one to break the silence of our ascent.

"If you don't say anything, it would be better," she advises. "He doesn't tend to like cops."

"We're both cops," I remind her. "Who are we here to see?"

Smith makes no effort to reply. When we arrive on the top floor, the elevator door creaks and groans in protest. For a second, I don't think it will actually open; it seems more likely that we're destined to meet our end by falling to the bottom of the elevator shaft. When it does finally jerk loudly ajar, I'm relieved to plant my feet firmly on the floor beyond. The room before us is well furnished and modern, a stark difference from the rest of the building. At the far end of the room, there's an outsize oak desk that's worth more than my house.

Seated in a high-backed red leather chair behind the desk is a sharply dressed man who looks to be in his early fifties. I recognize him as Adrian Smith, one of Motor City's most notorious mobsters. I turn my gaze briefly to Smith, wondering about the connection between her and Adrian, and about their shared last name. *That can't be a coincidence.* Her eyes meet mine, and she nods slightly as if to agree with my thoughts.

Adrian greets her warmly. "Shay! So nice to see you again! You hardly come by anymore."

She moves across the room to stand in front of the intimidating desk. I stay slightly behind her. She rests her palms on the dark oak surface and leans forward. "That's because I don't like you."

There's confidence and truth in her voice, but Adrian continues as if she hasn't said anything. "You look good. How's the job? Still fulfilling? Did you get the flowers I sent you on your birthday?"

"I got the flowers. I burned them, too. I'm not here to catch up. I'm here for business."

"That's a shame. It would be nice just to be a family for a change," Adrian says, almost pouting.

"You aren't my family, Adrian, you're just the asshole that happened to knock up my mother," Smith says flatly. There's deep-seated anger in her voice, the kind that can only come from a dark and chaotic past.

"That's no way to talk to your father, Shay," Adrian protests. "I have always been there for you."

"I don't want or need you in my life. What I want is some information."

"There's no winning with you, is there?" Adrian sighs. "You could have been anything you wanted to be. Why be a cop?"

There's genuine curiosity in his question. I too would like to know the answer.

"I'm a cop so one day, when you slip up, I can put you in your place, Adrian," Smith replies.

The tension is becoming thick enough that I'm starting to feel its weight. My mind is swirling so fast that I begin to feel dizzy. *My partner is the daughter of the roughest mobster in the state. Jesus, how can this day get any worse?*

Adrian sighs heavily and leans back in his chair, his frustration showing in the tense muscles of his face and neck. Smith's hands are clamped firmly on the edge of the desk. Her back is arched as if she's about to leap over it. I get ready to pull them off of each other if I need to.

Eventually, Smith breaks the silence. Her voice is both fire and ice. "I'm here for information, Adrian. Don't make me ask again."

"What would you do, Shay? We both know if you had anything on me you would have used it by now." Adrian's reply is calm.

Smith does not move a muscle. "I might not have anything to take you down with right now, but I could call in a raid on this building. I'm sure we wouldn't find anything useful, but I imagine that you'd lose a lot of money being shut down for twenty-four hours while we search."

She's using a bold tactic. I half expect Adrian to jump over the table and try to strangle her to death. After a few moments of agonizing tension, he says, "You wouldn't dare."

"Who do you think called in the last raid?" Smith says, glee and satisfaction in her voice.

Adrian contemplates this before responding. "You expect me to believe that the raid here last month was you?"

"I told you I hate flowers."

I flinch, expecting him to lose his temper completely at this point. Instead, a smile makes its way across his face.

"You are definitely my daughter. Every bit as stubborn and manipulative as I am. Fine. What do you want to know?"

"My partner and I are looking for someone who managed to hack into sophisticated surveillance equipment to cover their tracks. I need to know who could do that kind of thing. I need the name on the top of the hackers list."

Adrian takes a pen and notepad from a drawer in his desk. It's odd to see someone use such an archaic method, but I suppose it's safer than a smart desk. For a criminal in Motor City, leaving an electronic record could mean life or death. Better to have his most valuable information in his head instead of a computer. Adrian scrawls something on the notepad, tears off the page, and holds it out to Smith. She grabs it, but before he lets go, he says, "This is the name and address of an associate of mine. I'll tell him that you're coming to see him sometime tomorrow morning. He's a touchy person; hates cops more than I do. Be careful, and don't accuse him of anything."

"I'll accuse whoever I think is guilty."

"He isn't the guy you're looking for, Shay. He wouldn't leave enough evidence to get caught. He may know who you're looking for, though."

His point made, Adrian releases the piece of paper, and Smith folds it and puts it in her jacket pocket. She turns and walks past me toward the dilapidated elevator. I tear my shell-shocked gaze from Adrian and start to follow her, but before I get a foot in her direction, Adrian speaks up.

"Havoc, you mind sticking around?" His voice is deceptively casual.

As I pause, Smith gets into the elevator. Whatever comes next, I am to face on my own. Before the elevator doors close, I make sure that I still have my car keys in my jacket pocket. The last thing I need today is to be stranded in this part of town.

I turn back to Adrian. "I don't mind," I say in an feeble attempt to hide my concern.

"Good. Come have a seat." Adrian motions to a chair across the desk from him. I reluctantly move over to it and sit down. "How long have you been my daughter's partner, Havoc?"

"I'm not sure that's any of your business, Adrian," I say, trying to be both polite and firm.

"Shay is my daughter. It's my business to keep her safe."

I ponder his words. After deciding that he already knows how long we've been partners, I realize that how I answer the question is a test of my character.

"Partners since this morning."

"I'm impressed. You must have a decent head on your shoulders if she brought you with her to see me."

"She tried to steal my car to come see you. I sort of didn't have a choice but to come with her after that."

Adrian chuckles. "That's my girl! Well, let's keep things simple, then. She might be on the opposite side of things from me, but she will always be my daughter. I expect you to make sure she stays safe out there. That way, we can all rest easy." He's still using that deceptively casual tone.

"Are you threatening me, Adrian?"

"Of course not. Consider it a friendly understanding." With that, he holds his hand out for me to shake. I don't really want to. I figure it could be the death of me not to, though.

Mobsters can be touchy that way. It's a firm handshake, and before he lets go, he leans toward me and looks me right in the eye.

"Don't ever give me a reason to actually threaten you, Havoc. Understand?"

"I understand."

He releases my hand. I walk back to the elevator, turning to look at Adrian as the doors close. We lock eyes and hold the gaze until the ornate brass and metal doors come between us. In the lobby, I find Smith talking with Murray. They're laughing about something, probably me. Smith is having another cigarette. It takes a moment for her to notice me, and after she does, she says her goodbyes. I follow her silently out of the building, desperate to get back to the relative safety of the harsh streets.

Side by side, we walk across the road to the hearse. I'm relieved to see Elli undamaged. Now that I know whose building I parked across from, I understand why no one would mess with any of the cars on this part of the street. Smith drops her cigarette onto the sidewalk and grinds it out with her boot. Once we're both inside with the doors closed, I speak up.

"Well, now I understand why you didn't want me to come with you."

"It doesn't exactly sit well with people that I'm his daughter," Smith says with the first hint of embarrassment I've heard from her.

"Why be a cop? Adrian has more money than God," I say, still in a state of shock.

"I'm not even going to answer that, Havoc. I took the same tests you did. I became a cop because that was what the system demanded I become. I continue to be a cop to put a stop to people like Adrian."

"Well, I admire your devotion."

"It isn't devotion, Havoc. Nobody gets to choose who their parents are. That asshole's drugs are what got my mother hooked. He made her into a Tech junkie for life, and he doesn't even feel guilty about it."

"That's messed up. Sorry," I say, knowing I've stepped across a line again.

"Nothing you can do to change it, Havoc. Why should you care, anyway?"

I open my mouth to respond, but then think better of it. There's no need to make things worse than they already are.

I start up Elli and pull out onto the road. I waste no time getting as far away from this side of town as possible. After a while spent in awkward silence, which is quickly becoming a theme for us, I decide to ask Smith if she wants me to take her home. We're still a few miles from the department. "Can I give you a ride back to your place?"

"Sure, I guess. Take a right at the next light. A left two blocks ahead from there."

I follow her instructions and end up at a massive apartment building. It's not the best part of town to live in, but it's nicer than my neighborhood. *I bet Smith doesn't even have to wake up to the sound of gunfire more than once every few weeks,* I think. I imagine that would be quite refreshing. She has me pull over on other the side of the street from her building.

"You want a ride to the department in the morning?" I ask. "I don't live too far from here. Just a block off of Hastings Street."

"If you want to. Sure."

Smith checks her pockets, probably to be sure she has her cigarettes and lighter. Then she opens the door and slides out of the Cadillac in one fluid motion. Once she's out, she turns back and leans in through the half-open door. "Thanks."

"For the ride? Don't worry about it. I'd just prefer it if you ask before borrowing my car next time."

"I mean thanks for not completely freaking out that my father's Adrian Smith."

I'm tempted to scream, "Of course I'm freaked out about who your father is!" Adrian has become another potential method on a growing list of things Motor City could use to kill me. I hold back my discomfort and choose my words with care. "It's like you said, we can't choose our parents. See you in the morning."

She closes the car door and walks off. I stay for a minute to make sure she gets in OK. It's more habit than necessity; Smith is clearly capable of taking care of herself. Once she's inside, I pull out and head for home.

The short drive gives me enough time to ponder the gravity of all that has happened in just a single day. At least I feel as if Smith doesn't hate me quite as much as when the day started. I will definitely have to keep a close watch on my car keys in the future, although the discovery that her father is Adrian Smith has much more unsettling potential consequences than the thought of her trying to take my car again.

As I pull into the driveway of my run-down Victorian house, I'm glad to see the lights on inside. Rina is home. I'm desperately looking forward to a quiet evening away from the craziness of my first day as a detective.

I find Rina at the kitchen table. She's munching on a bowl of cereal, surrounded by her schoolbooks.

"Looks like you're having fun."

Rina looks up from her studies. She smirks and says, "Yeah, something like that. How was your first day?" She closes the book in front of her and rests an elbow on it, looking at me expectantly as I sit down. I can tell she's craving a recap. I decide to give her a brief description to appease her curiosity.

"Turns out Chief Anderson made me lead detective."

"Well, that's impressive," she says, nodding.

"I suppose. Except my new partner was looking to get the job too."

"Oh. Awkward."

"Yeah, she doesn't seem to like me that much. I guess that's why she tried to steal my car."

"Whoa, double awkward," Rina says, this time shaking her head.

"No shit. On top of all of that, our first case is a real tricky murder."

I'm tempted to reveal that my partner's father is a mob boss. It would be nice to get that off my chest. But I hold that piece of information back. There are some things that Rina is better off not knowing. The identity of Smith's father is definitely one of them, at least for now, anyway.

"Jeez, sounds like one hell of a first day," she says.

"Yeah. How was yours?"

"Same old. Nothing quite as exciting as schoolwork. Hopefully all of this knowledge keeps me out of law enforcement. Otherwise, it's a really shitty way to waste my time," she says with a dry chuckle.

"I think what you're doing beats the six hours my partner and I spent watching surveillance footage."

"Wow. You really did cover all of the bases today, didn't you?"

I give her a rueful nod and a smile.

I decide I might as well join Rina and have cereal for dinner. Each of us has a couple of bowls, and we talk and laugh for a while. I help her study and then call it an early night. Not only do I need to be up earlier than usual to pick up Smith, I also need to have a meeting with all of the other detectives first thing. Before bed, I look over the information from the cases that they're working on. As reading goes, it's pretty dry, and sadly for me, most of the department seems to be doing better than I am.

Eventually, I fall asleep with my transponder still in my hand. My sleep is uneasy, and I dream of dark things, painful memories. I'm glad not to remember their exact details when I awaken. My eyes fly open a few minutes before my alarm goes off. There's cold sweat on my forehead, and my heart is racing. Outside the window, the streets of Motor City are eerily quiet.

CHAPTER 6

DISTRACTION

I dress myself in my nicest black jeans and a dark gray button-up shirt. I finish off the outfit with my dark red tie, the most formal thing I have. Clipping the detective badge to my belt feels surreal, almost as if I stole it. A rush of painful irony washes over me as I realize that I would prefer to have my old job back. The pay sucked, and I never expected to live through the day, but somehow that seems better than my new position. *Maybe it's just because I was used to it,* I tell myself. *If I can push past these first few days and weeks and establish a routine, everything will seem less chaotic.* I double check my gun and ensure that I have extra ammo. It's becoming a nervous habit. After what happened on my first day as lead detective, I would rather go back into that building with Ramirez than face the rest of the detectives this morning. I take a deep breath as I look in the mirror.

"You can do this."

I say it to myself as encouragement, but instead, it makes me feel even more strange. Being a leader is not something I wanted. I've always thought of myself as a follower. I go downstairs and have a quick bite of breakfast with Rina before I head out. I get in the old Cadillac and fire her up. At least Elli doesn't change. That's about the only comfort I have to hold onto right now. The big hearse lumbers down the street toward Smith's apartment.

When I get there, I realize that I never asked for her transponder number. I shut down the hearse and lock her up. Making my way to the entrance of Smith's building, I continue to worry about the coming speech. *I'm going to fuck it up, I know I am.* I press the call button on the touch screen by the door and say Smith's full name. After a moment of searching, the screen patches me through to her apartment.

It rings several times with no answer. I check the time on my transponder. *Shit, I'm early; she's going to kill me.* Finally, on what is likely the last ring, Smith's face appears on the screen.

"What do you want?" she asks, eyes red and narrow.

"It's Havoc, your partner, remember? I'm here to pick you up."

My call to the apartment has obviously woken her up. Her hair is even more disheveled than it was yesterday. She keeps blinking periodically to avoid the brightness of her in-room screen. She thinks about my words, processing them as if I was speaking a foreign language, then says, "Right. I'll buzz you up. Fourth floor, apartment four ten."

Her face disappears from the screen, and the front door clicks open. I enter the narrow lobby and take the elevator at the end up to the fourth floor. The elevator's speaker is wonky, making the annoying jingle that's playing come across as a staticky mess. With a quick scan of the room numbers, I find Smith's apartment at the end of the corridor. I press the talk button on the screen.

"It's Havoc."

No answer.

"Should I come in?"

Though Smith's face doesn't appear on the screen, her voice replies from a distance. "It's unlocked, come in."

I'm not surprised to see that it's a fairly decent-sized studio apartment. She's on her own, so she has fewer living expenses than I do, and she's been working Homicide for a while. The room, however, is in a state of chaos. Clothes are all over the place. *Has she ever heard of a laundry basket?* There are knickknacks on every surface not inhabited by discarded garments. The walls are covered with brightly colored paint contrasted by dark paintings and drawings. She has quite the talent for art, assuming they're her creations. I can smell cigarette smoke despite how illegal it would be for her to be smoking inside her apartment. The curtains on the windows at the far end of the room are tightly drawn, making the interior murky. Slivers of light slip through them, revealing a floor on which there are only a few bare spots.

Smith is seated on the edge of the bed, facing the wall of curtains. Slumped over, she appears to be tying her boots.

"You're early." She sounds more than slightly annoyed.

"I thought it was better than being late."

"I think I preferred you late," she says shortly.

She stands up and stretches, then walks over to a dresser opposite the bed, the left side of her body facing me. She fumbles through the drawers and eventually produces a shirt and bra. With no warning, she removes her shirt and starts changing into the new clothes, exposing one nicely contoured breast. Startled, I turn too late to avoid seeing her disrobe. I feel both self-conscious and profoundly uncomfortable. This is inappropriate at best, and the fact that I'm Shay's superior makes it even worse. But if I report it to HR, there will be serious repercussions for both of us; plus, I'll be buried under a pile of paperwork.

When she's finished getting changed, Smith brushes by me and takes her jacket from the wall by the door.

"Are you coming?" she asks.

I follow her. It's as if she doesn't care that I just saw her half naked. I feel awkward enough that I make no attempt at conversation on our way to the car. Even enduring the steady rasp of static from the elevator speaker is preferable to speaking. Outside, we pile into Elli and head for the department.

About halfway there, and still no conversation. Smith takes out a cigarette. I roll my eyes at her, but she doesn't notice.

"I'd rather you didn't smoke in my car," I say.

"Yeah? Well, I'd rather my partner didn't stare at my tits while I get dressed."

Her comment puts me at a loss for words, which could have been her intention from the start. *Can she really be that manipulative? Or was she just being oblivious?* Either way, I'm disappointed. After last night's parting words, I thought we were getting close to a more solid partnership. Now we're worse off than when we started. She lights her cigarette and rolls down the window. I'm left to contemplate whether or not she planned to have me see her half naked. If so, she's using it against me. If not, she's taking advantage of an opportunity. Either way, I'm getting fed up with her actions. I turn up the radio to let the local station distract me from my anger. They play a few songs from PBX, the band Rina and I saw at the park.

We arrive, and I park the hearse in its spot in the garage. There's still no conversation between us. Smith walks silently beside me, chewing on a sucker to replace the cigarette. In the building, near the Homicide Division, I'm a little alarmed when she finally starts to talk to me.

"I really messed with your head on the whole tits thing, didn't I? This is the quietest you've been since we met," Smith says, bemused by my silence.

"People don't generally take their shirt off in front of me."

I realize how embarrassing my statement is as the words spill out. Before I have a chance to explain myself, she chimes in with a devilish grin, "Really? Shame."

We reach the entry for Homicide Division, which cuts our conversation short. There are fifty homicide detective positions, and they're highly coveted; someone had to have retired or died for me to get one. With two detectives on each case, it makes for as many as twenty-five ongoing homicide cases at any given time. My desk is at the front of the large office. Smith's is to the right of mine. As I take my place behind my desk, forty-nine pairs of eyes watch me expectantly. I swallow hard and push past my nerves.

"I'm sure you all know my name by now. You can call me Harvey if you like. I prefer to keep things informal. I know you are all capable detectives or you wouldn't be here. I'm going to make things simple. If you have questions or problems, let me know. Other than that, I'd appreciate a brief report on your cases at the end of each week. I trust all of you to do your jobs. I expect results as fast as you can manage them. Let's be safe out there. We all know Motor City's ugly side."

Most of the detectives seem to take in my words, but I can tell that several stopped paying attention right after I began to speak. As the crowd disperses to their assigned casework, Walt comes up to greet me and Smith.

"I see you two haven't killed each other yet," he says.

"Not for lack of trying." Smith says this with triumph in her voice and a big grin on her face.

Walt chuckles at her remark, then directs his next statement to me. "That was a nice speech. Don't think I remember the last time so many of the detectives actually paid attention to the lead."

"Thanks."

"You two have any luck with your case yet?" he asks, eyeing us both.

"Not much," Smith admits. "We've got to go check in with a contact today. See if we can shake out something worthwhile."

"Ah. Well, good luck to you both." Walk turns his head to look me in the eye. "I have a recommendation for you, Havoc."

"What?" I ask, concerned by his focus.

"If you don't want her to continue taking your car, get hers fixed."

"How'd you know about that?" I ask, exasperated.

"She took my car on our first day as partners too. See you both around."

He winks at me before leaving the room. Smith is looking at me from the corner of her eye, a smirk still on her face. I try to ignore this while I take a quick look through the information on the other detectives' cases. When I'm done with my smart desk, I shut it off and head for the garage. Shay follows me.

"You really enjoy making things difficult, don't you?" I ask my partner before I start up the hearse.

"I like to think of it as keeping people on their toes. Besides, it's always easier to give a good speech when you're distracted," Smith says matter-of-factly.

"First you use me seeing you with your shirt off as an excuse to smoke in my car. Now you're telling me it helped me give a good speech? You're insane. Something like this could get me fired, or worse, demoted all the way back to Street Division!"

"It distracted you. I see that as a success," Smith says, her devilish grin returning.

"Yesterday you hate my guts. Today you're trying to help me by taking off your shirt? You are the strangest, most frustrating partner I've ever had."

"Aw, thanks," Smith says, batting her eyelashes.

I shake my head and start up the hearse, and Smith enters the hacker's address into the dashboard GPS. As we head out, I cannot help but wonder what kind of trouble Smith is going to get me into today. At least she's not smoking this time. Perhaps she's decided to give me a break, or perhaps she has more of a sweet tooth for suckers than a craving for nicotine.

The address is an apartment complex nestled in the heart of Motor City's industrial zone. The smell of the factories permeates the air. As we walk over to the suspect's building, I contemplate the area's history. In the early part of the new century, a large number of technical industries moved into Motor City along with the vehicle remanufacturing industry, taking advantage of the low cost of property and labor. In a way, it was a marvelous reincarnation of Motor City. However, more industry means more people, and more people inevitably leads to more crime. I'd imagine that Adrian Smith started out as a low-level street thug. Motor City industry's aggressive growth allowed him and many others like him to carve out a piece of the action.

"Our guy's name is Jasper Collins," Smith says, snapping me out of my reverie. "I pulled his record last night after work. Looks like he has a list of charges a mile long. No convictions."

"He must have a great lawyer."

"In the line of work he's in, I'm sure he can afford the best."

Smith's brief description is enough to tell me the kind of person we're about to deal with. If you want to be a criminal these days, your best shot at success is to play the game correctly. Those who are smart enough allow themselves to be arrested quietly whenever they're under suspicion of a crime. From there, if they cover their tracks well enough, a good lawyer can get them off fairly quickly. Evading the law this long gives types like Jasper a god complex. It's unlikely that he had anything to do with tampering with the camera on May's street. A guy like him would've used footage that was almost identical to what was erased. The mistake with the flag movement suggests that it was a rushed cover-up or the work of an amateur.

I follow Smith toward the apartment building, as she has Jasper's information loaded on the screen of her transponder. She calls his room number on the touch screen by the front door. I'm not surprised to see the face of a young man, probably no more than twenty, come into view. Disheveled, medium-length, dark brown hair falls over his eyes. It looks as if he has neglected to shave for at least a week.

"What do you want?" He sounds annoyed and suspicious.

"My name is Shay Smith. This is my partner, Havoc. Adrian sent us to speak with you. He said he'd let you know we were coming."

I'm impressed with the way Smith speaks to Jasper. Unlike her interaction with the apartment manager yesterday morning, there is respect in her voice. I cannot decide if this is because she wants Jasper to feel comfortable with her or if it's because she thinks she's talking to someone more on her level than I am.

"Ah, you're Adrian's kid. Just give me a minute and I'll buzz you up," Jasper says.

His face disappears from the screen. Smith and I wait in silence. Jasper is no doubt taking the opportunity to put away anything that a detective shouldn't see. I can only imagine the sort of people he's working for; likely a who's who of Motor City's foulest scum.

A few moments later, the door clicks open. This is an older apartment building. There's no elevator, only a sparsely decorated entryway and a staircase leading up to the higher floors. The apartment complex is an excellent time capsule of 1980s design, with large cast-concrete walls and pillars, exposed utilities, and dull tones. I follow Smith as she makes her way up the cast-concrete staircase.

"You ever met this kid before?" I ask.

"Nope," Smith says.

Her simple one-word reply is the extent of our conversation until we make it to the fifth floor of the apartment building. We walk down a long corridor and come to Jasper's apartment on the left side of the hall, about halfway down. Smith calls in on his touch screen, and his face appears on it briefly as he confirms that it's us. There's a series of extra clicks in the process of the door opening, indicating that he has added extra security. It's odd that someone who makes as much as Jasper likely does would live in a run-down apartment complex in the industrial zone. Maybe he feels safer in keeping a low profile. Or perhaps he chooses to live cheaply to make a greater profit. An apartment like his probably costs a third of what Smith's studio does.

Jasper is waiting for us just inside the door. It doesn't take long to realize that he hasn't showered in a while. He's wearing a white T-shirt with the words "FUCK OFF!" on it in bright red neon letters and a small PBX logo on the bottom hem. Jeans and house slippers complete his nonchalant ensemble. He would've fit right in at the punk concert. The light from an LED is shining through the matted hair by his right ear. He has some kind of communication device in his ear, possibly even an implant.

Many different types of communication equipment is scattered around the large apartment. Cables and cords snake their way around the edge of the floor in a confusing mass. Empty coffee cups from Super K are scattered on almost every surface. I note that most of the equipment is available to the average person at a high price. Some of the servers are harder to come by for civilian use. He would have had to pull some special strings to get the permits for them.

"Have a fuckin' seat if you like," Jasper says as he motions to a couple of old folding chairs near a group of servers. He sits down in a comfortable-looking adjustable office chair. Behind him is a daunting wall of screens. Some of them are showing news feeds. Others show lines of code. A few are sporting the cheesy image of a skull and crossbones as a screen saver. There's a touch screen keyboard attached to the arm of his chair.

"Adrian tells me you're looking for some smartass with the knowledge to hack into police surveillance. You pigs bring a sample of the altered footage?" Jasper asks, flipping the hair out of his face with a shake of his head.

I feel a tinge of frustration as I realize that I didn't remember to record a sample of the footage on my transponder. I was too busy worrying about Smith trying to steal my car. All too happy to once again outclass me, Smith pulls out her transponder.

"You got an address I can send it to?" she asks, her tone still polite.

Jasper rattles off a long string of numbers and letters. Once Smith has finished sending him the footage, he turns to the wall of screens, pulls it up on the largest of them, and views the two separate clips with great concentration. After playing each a few times, he turns back to speak with us.

"It's a fucking rad splice, technically speaking. The transition between frames is almost prefect; they just used shitty footage to overlay it. They would've been better off cloning the original footage rather than screwing themselves by splicing in footage from a different night."

"How'd you know it was from a different night?" I ask. "It could've been from earlier in the evening."

Jasper smiles condescendingly, proud to outwit a cop so easily. "You'd think so. The lighting is too good for that, though. If it was footage from earlier, there would've been subtle lighting differences. My guess is that it was from the night before at the same time. Let me check my theory."

He turns back to the wall of screens and opens a feed for the weather patterns around Motor City over the last few days. "When did this shit happen?" he asks.

"Night before last," Smith answers.

He looks up the date and taps a few more keys, and I realize he's looking at wind records. After a few minutes of searching, he says, "Yep, I'm seeing mild winds in the area on the night before your crime. I'd bet your guy hacked the camera station that night for the footage. Then he came back the next night to do the deed and spliced it in before the scheduled download."

"You got any names for us?" Smith says hopefully, still polite.

He scrawls down a few names on a notepad, tears off the page, and holds it out to her, a strange echo of Adrian's actions the day before. "These are the most likely douchebags."

"Wouldn't it be better to check your records?" Smith sounds concerned.

Jasper smiles at her comment, then chuckles. He raises a finger to the side of his head. "Some records are best kept here."

"Generous of you to give us the info, Jasper. Thanks," I say.

Jasper turns to face me. A crooked grin makes its way across his pale lips. "I never work for free, Havoc."

"You can't expect us to pay you, Jasper. We're police," Smith says, sounding annoyed with him for the first time.

Jasper turns back to her, grinning even more widely. "No worries. Your daddy already paid me for it," he hisses.

I see the look in Smith's eyes change. The civility is gone, replaced by fiery disgust. Wordlessly, she stands and walks out of the room, her boots falling hard against the floor. I get up to follow her. Behind me, I hear Jasper's parting shot. "I guess I upset daddy's little girl."

I'm glad that Smith is out of earshot. I get the impression that if she had heard him, there would soon be a CSI crew trying to scrape Jasper's brains off of his wall of screens. I have to run to catch up with her; she's already down the first flight of stairs.

"You OK?" I ask.

"Does it fucking look like it?" she yells.

"How we got the info doesn't matter. Just that we have it."

Smith stops on the stair just below me and turns to glare at me. "It matters to me."

With that, she continues down the staircase. I follow in silence. As we drive off in the Cadillac, she takes out a cigarette. I decide not to bother her about it. She has enough on her mind already, and I have no intention of being in her line of fire. Noticing the time, I decide to go by a Speedy Sam's sandwich kiosk near the department. Maybe lunch will help take her mind off things.

There's no talk between us throughout the process of getting food. Smith takes her sandwich from me and gazes off into the distance beyond the vast hood of the Cadillac. It's impossible to tell if she's looking at something in particular or is just focused on her thoughts.

I park Elli on a side street few blocks from the department. This way, we can eat in peace, uninterrupted by the gossip of the department cafeteria. Smith eats without looking at her food, still staring into the distance. I find myself thinking what a curse it must be for her to have a father like Adrian. The money and the security would be nice, I suppose. The rest would quickly wear down even the strongest person. Even though my own parents are dead, I feel that I'm luckier than she is. After finishing my sandwich, I decide it's as good a time as any to try to break the ice.

"Is your blue hair natural?" I ask.

"Huh?" Smith says, coming back to reality.

"Well, I was talking to the department narcotics expert a while back, and she said that unique hair colors could come from children born of Tech users."

"Oh, yeah. I know Anteka. I've talked to her about it before," Smith says.

"So it's naturally that color, then?"

"Yeah. My mother had a tattoo of a blue orchid. She almost OD'd on Tech when she was pregnant with me."

"That's wild."

"I guess," Smith says dismissively.

Realizing I might be delving too far into topics she doesn't want to bring up, I change tack. "You up to talking to a couple of the people on Jasper's list?" I ask.

At first, it's as if I've said nothing at all. A moment or two later, I'm concerned that I've said too much. A few more tense seconds pass before Smith processes my words enough to form a reply. "Yeah. We should."

"You doing OK? Seems like you've been off in another world for the last half hour."

"I'm fine."

Her lie is as halfhearted as her engagement with the world around her. Despite her distraction, she manages to look up the names Jasper provided on her transponder and put the next address into the dashboard GPS. I fire up the V8 and pull the big hearse back onto the main road.

I follow the pleasant voice of Elli's GPS to a neighborhood several blocks over, a collection of houses rather than apartments. The modern homes and duplexes are so pristine that they're almost sterile, a far cry from the dwellings that used to occupy the area. I remember it as a slum from when I was a small boy.

Many slum neighborhoods were demolished in the early 2040s to make room for new housing. There was a certain idealistic hope for the future at the time these neighborhoods were built. What was idealism then now seems to be just a facade. The modern homes look out of place somehow, as if the future failed to live up to their standards. I pull up to the curb alongside the house designated by the GPS and shut the engine off.

I suppose if you were to take someone from the late twentieth century and drop them in front of a house like this, they would believe in the magic of the future. It's a prime example of modern architecture mixed with the latest technology, a clean steel and glass structure with strong brick accents, dark colors, and smooth fixtures. Minimal in design. Bland in style.

"This is an awfully nice place for a low-level hacker."

My words fall on deaf ears. Smith is still off in her own head somewhere. I notice that there's no sound of nearby gunfire, likely because this neighborhood is higher-class and close to MCPD headquarters. It's almost too quiet for Motor City. I realize with a certain disgust that the crook we are about to meet probably makes more money in a day than I do in a month.

Smith gets out of the Cadillac. I follow her down the short driveway to the front of the house. On our way, I notice a small camera pod near the front door. I'm betting that our presence has been noted since I parked on the street. Smith is still distant, so I engage the call pad next to the door. The face of a man who appears to be in his mid-thirties appears on the screen. He has black hair and deeply tanned skin, a medium-length beard, and pale brown eyes. I assume he's the owner of the first name on our list, Bill Huxley.

"What can I do for you officers?" the man says pleasantly.

My assumption about him watching us is confirmed by his question. Our walk up to the door gave him ample time to spot the bar codes on the sides of our heads and use his hacking skills to find out some basic information about us.

"Bill Huxley?" I verify. When he nods, I say, "We would like a few moments of your time."

During this exchange, Smith's gaze remains distant, her posture relaxed.

"Fine. I have some time. Come in," Huxley says.

The door clicks open, and he lets us into his home. The furnishings inside match the outside, modern and clean. His wardrobe is as immaculate and generic as his home. Unlike Jasper's place, it's hard to tell from the surroundings that Huxley is a hacker. There aren't computer towers everywhere, and there are no rat's nests of cords to trip on. The only clear sign is that he can afford to be home, in this neighborhood, on a Tuesday afternoon.

He leads us to a nicely furnished living room and has us sit down. I can't tell if Smith feels as awkward as I do to be in such a fine home, though she does appear to be stepping lightly on the off-white carpet. At least our surroundings seem to be dragging her thoughts back into the present.

"Can I get you anything? Coffee, perhaps?" Huxley asks, wonderfully more polite than Jasper.

"No, thanks. We aren't going to be here long. Just a few questions," Smith says. I'm relieved to see her reengage with our case.

"Ah … what sort of questions?"

"Are you an experienced hacker?" Smith asks, turning on her transponder's record feature.

I can see the distaste Huxley has for the term hacker written on his face. He also looks annoyed by Smith's directness. "I work with a number of different technologies, some in the professional field and some privately."

His attempt at deflection does not impress Smith. Her reply has a hostile tone. "Do you know how to tamper with surveillance footage from the Motor City Police Department, for example?"

"I could in theory. It isn't worth the risk," Huxley replies shortly.

I decide to chime in, hoping to ease the tension. "Would you mind if we looked through your server just to be sure?"

Huxley directs his next statement to me. "You're welcome to get a warrant order sent over from the department for that if you like. Or I could save you the time. I have the skills, sure; I've never done anything below board, though. My clients pay me well because I know how to operate with the law in mind."

Despite his recommendation, Smith stops recording and fills out the necessary information for a warrant order on her transponder's screen. After a few minutes of waiting for the on-duty judge to sign it remotely, she's ready for Huxley to sign it with his fingerprint. Smith and I also sign the warrant order. Huxley wastes no time setting us up with his server, and we perform an in-depth scan of his data. As he predicted, we waste an hour looking for anything suspicious. Smith leaves without engaging him further. I briefly thank him and follow her out to the hearse. Once we're both inside, I break the silent tension.

"Do you want to go talk with the other names on the list? Or should we take a break on this till tomorrow?"

Smith has been staring into the distance again, but snaps out of it more quickly than I anticipated. "Sure. Let's get a few more names crossed off the list."

CHAPTER 9

HACKERS

After adding more addresses to the GPS, we leave Huxley's quaint neighborhood. The next name on our short list takes us to one of the highest-end neighborhoods in Motor City. It features several of the oldest and most carefully restored homes. Some of the wealthiest families of our fair city reside here in just a few square blocks. As we enter the neighborhood, I wonder if it's the kind of place Chief Anderson would live. On recalling that there were no family pictures in his office, I think better of my theory. *Anderson probably lives in a fancy apartment, maybe something similar to where May lived. Possibly even nicer than that.* Pushing these random thoughts to the back of my mind, I focus on the moment.

I pull up to the curb across the street from a home matching the address on my screen. It's an imposing four-story brick house. The design suggests it was originally built in the early 1900s. My old hearse must stand out in strange contrast to its formal aesthetic. As I shut down the engine, I get a chill down my spine. A glance toward the stately home confirms my suspicion. I see a face at a window on the second floor, but it disappears behind a curtain before I can distinguish any features. Smith followed my glance toward the house, and her words validate my vision.

"Well, someone knows we're here."

We get out of the hearse and walk toward the door. A large, ancient oak tree casts a long shadow across the front lawn and the walkway leading to the home. I instinctively scan the area, looking for any movement. Nothing is out of place; it's perfect cookie-cutter bliss as far as I can see. The maintenance alone for such a property outweighs the cost of my monthly rent.

"You think there's any point in talking to this one? Judging by the looks of this place, he doesn't need to hack to make a living," I say.

"With a place like this, he can probably do whatever he wants. I'd say it's a veritable breeding ground for a hacker," Smith replies.

We walk up the front steps toward the large door. Its color is close to the shade of my tie. A call screen has been fitted into the brickwork on the wall next to the door. There's a screen saver on it to help mask its presence. It's a family crest, the surname Kelly at the top of a shield flanked by lions. As we stop in front of the door, the crest disappears, revealing the face of young Brandon Kelly.

His face is quite thin, his skin so pale that I doubt he ever sees sunlight. His dark brown hair is carefully combed, his eyes a pale green. I consider the disappointing likelihood that I'm looking at a future leader of our city. No doubt his youthful indiscretions will be swept under the rug and a fast track to becoming a politician will take the place of his hacking pursuits.

"Are you Brandon Kelly?" Smith asks.

"Yes. What do you want?" says Brandon, eyes narrowed.

"We're detectives, just have a few quick questions for you."

His eyes dart from Smith to me and back again. I start to think we don't have a chance of even getting through the door. His face disappears from the screen and is replaced with the Kelly crest. The door clicks open. He stands behind it as we enter, only his face protruding around its edge. Brandon is tall for his age, almost my height. The mousy young man motions us to a sitting room near the foyer.

Shay and I seat ourselves gingerly on the edge of a lavish sofa. Brandon treats himself to a large velvet-covered armchair. There's not one single item out of place. Not a speck of dust on any horizontal surface. This is the polar opposite of Jasper's apartment. I haven't even seen any technology besides the front door call screen.

"What can I help you with?" Brandon asks, shifting to the edge of his chair with his hands folded.

"We're looking into a few hackers in the Motor City area. Your name popped up," Smith says, starting to record with her transponder.

"It's just a hobby of mine. I never work for anyone."

"Would you mind if we took a look at your system?" Smith asks with what I can tell is forced politeness.

"Yes," Brandon says definitively.

"We can get a warrant," Smith says, holding her ground.

"I doubt it," Brandon replies with a crooked smirk. He stands up abruptly and points toward the door. "I would like you to leave now."

Smith stands and leans forward, getting her face within a few inches of Brandon's. He leans back. He clearly did not expect her to call his bluff. The wind leaves his sails, and he sinks back into his chair. Smith sticks with him, keeping her face close to his.

"Just because you get whatever you want doesn't make you immune to the law. Maybe one day you'll test into the force like I did. Mommy and Daddy can't protect you forever," she says, shoving her index finger in his face.

Brandon's reply is meek, almost too quiet to hear. "Get out."

Smith storms off, every bootfall echoing across the vast house. I leave without another word. Smith is already in the car and ready to go by the time I get there. With a bit of luck, maybe young Brandon Kelly will be too frightened to file a complaint against her. I need that on my first week as lead detective like I need a hole in my head. We're burning through suspects as fast as Smith is running through her pack of cigarettes.

I decide not to confront her about her reaction to Brandon and concentrate on getting us out of the high-end neighborhood as fast as I dare to go. It's unlikely that we'll have any further contact with Brandon Kelly. Even if he did have something to do with the altered footage, we would have more luck pinning it on someone else than proving it was him.

We make our way back to the other side of town. Our next name is Doran Atkin. His apartment is above an old Irish pub downtown. Since it's now late afternoon, parking is a dismal prospect. I cruise the area at least half a dozen times before finding a spot large enough for the hearse. We have to walk a block and a half to get to the pub.

Here the streets are a sea of disgruntled and suspicious people. When I was a civilian, people would walk past me without a second glance, but now that I'm a cop, they tend to give me a wide berth. Making our way to the pub, we part the herd of distant faces and drab colors. It's as if there's a force field around us, keeping everyone at a distance. I notice a young man in a pale blue hoodie who fits Atkin's description coming down the side stairs on the building ahead. I nod in that direction, and Smith spots him as well.

He's tall and muscular, with deep brown skin, and as we get closer, I can't help but be a little intimidated by his stature. Atkin has short black hair and a frame built for survival in Motor City—or anywhere, for that matter. He notices us and pauses two stairs shy of the pavement, which adds another foot to his considerable height.

"Doran Atkin? Have a few questions for you."

It's as if my words flip a switch. In one fluid motion, Atkin descends the last two stairs and lands a solid punch to my nose, then darts down the dark alley. I stagger backward, cupping my hand over my nose as the blood runs down my upper lip. *Perfect, now my good shirt and tie have bloodstains on them,* I think dazedly. Smith has disappeared. I waste no time trying to figure out where she went and run down the alley after Atkin. Though we may be matched in strength, Atkin's long legs grant him a more impressive stride. It's all I can do just to trail behind him by several yards. He takes advantage of another alleyway to the right and ducks into it. As I come around the corner, I see him fall to the ground face-first. Smith has flanked him from the other side of the building, tripping him when he came around the corner.

Before Atkin can regain his footing, I'm on him with a pair of handcuffs. He swears as I clench them around his wrists. When his hands are secured behind his back, I help him up from the pavement. His nose is bleeding more aggressively than mine. The fall to the pavement proved more effective on him than his fist was on my face.

"I didn't have anything to do with what happened to Al, man!" Atkin yells.

"Al? You know what he's talking about, Smith?"

"No clue. I don't think I've ever known anyone named Al," Smith says.

Some of the fear leaves Atkin's face. He raises an eyebrow, though his body doesn't relax. "What you wanna talk to me for, then?" he asks, shaking his head.

"We're talking to hackers." I pull a handkerchief from my jacket and hold it to my nose. The pain has dulled somewhat. I doubt it's broken, but my shirt and tie are definitely done for.

"Shit, man, I sold off all my stuff a month ago. Had to pay the rent on this fuckin' dump," Atkin says.

"Why hit my partner and run?" Smith asks, unimpressed by his story.

"You serious?" He looks at her incredulously. "I'm a black man in Motor City. What the hell I'm gonna do when two white cops are comin' at me? Wait around to get sho—"

Smith cuts him off. "Just show us your goddamn apartment."

She grabs Atkin by the shoulder and ushers him back toward his building. I walk a little way behind them, still holding the handkerchief firmly to my nose. Seeing Smith escort Atkin is an interesting spectacle. He's at least a foot and a half taller than her, but her sharp, long fingers are digging into his shoulder, and he's slouching to the side she's gripping, indicating the high level of discomfort he's in.

We climb the staircase to his apartment with Atkin in the lead. Smith's grip does not falter as we continue to the landing. The blood flow from my nose has subsided. I fold the soiled handkerchief before returning it to my pocket.

"Keys," Smith says sharply.

"Front pocket of my sweatshirt," says Atkin.

Without releasing her grip on him, Smith uses her left hand to find the keys in his hoodie, then unlocks the door. There's no call screen by it. This must not be a legal apartment. If I cared enough, I could report it to the department. The pub owner would be stuck with a heavy fine for his illegal housing. The door swings inward, and we enter.

Smith shoves Atkin into a nearby armchair and begins to survey the dank apartment. I keep an eye on him as she searches the poorly lit rooms. Judging from what I can see, he has indeed sold all of his equipment. There's barely anything in the living room beyond an ancient TV and a few moldy chairs. After a short time, Smith returns, shaking her head.

"Anything?" I ask, trying to be hopeful.

"Nope. Why did you sell your shit, Atkin?" she asks, locking eyes with him.

"I *told* you. I had to pay the rent on this shithole," Atkin says with irritation.

"I could arrest you for hitting my partner," Smith says, crossing her arms. "That's assaulting an officer."

"Come on, I didn't mean it. This whole damn thing is just a stupid misunderstanding," Atkin says. He's trying to be cool, but he's shifting in his seat and glancing back and forth between us.

Smith's eyes dart to me. I shake my head. It isn't worth our time to mess with him any further. I can't say I blame him for hitting me, anyway; I imagine his previous encounters with cops haven't ended well for him. His punch was an act of self-defense, nothing more.

"You're lucky, Atkin. If you would've hit me like that, I would've stuck you in jail and slapped you with a fine so high you wouldn't have a shithole apartment to come back to," Smith says. She leaves the room. I hear her rapidly descending the staircase outside.

I turn to Atkin. "Stand up and turn around."

He awkwardly stands up and turns his back to me. I hesitate before releasing him from the cuffs, hoping he doesn't decide to try anything. When his hands are free, he turns around, and I raise my right hand slowly in a fist toward him.

"Sorry about your nose, man," I say.

He eyes me suspiciously, stares at my fist, shakes his head, then reluctantly bumps his knuckles against mine, saying, "This right here is the whitest bullshit I've ever participated in. Man, you're crazy."

There's not much I can say to that, so I just smile and nod in agreement, then make my way back to the hearse. I find Smith propped up by the front fender on the passenger side. She's taking the opportunity to have another cigarette.

"Your nose OK?" she asks, taking a long drag.

"I'm fine."

She shrugs and lets the final puff of smoke escape her lips before dropping the spent butt to the pavement. It meets a violent and definitive end beneath the heel of her boot. We get back into the hearse, and I dig out a bottle of water from behind the seat and remove a rag from the glove box. I wet the rag and use the rear-view mirror to clean the dried blood from my face. I try to clean my shirt and tie too, but it's no use.

Five blocks over, we meet our next suspect, Clay Kingston. Kingston is a weasel-faced man, and what he lacks in height, he more than makes up for in width. His shitty little apartment is across the road from a seedy strip club. Kingston greets us at the door wearing a plaid robe and the aroma of fried food. After the short, slimy bastard tells Smith, "I'd rather see you in my bed than in my server," there's little I can do to stop her. A strong right hook to Kingston's nose, continuing the day's theme, sends him to the floor.

He continues to complain and snivel as he signs a warrant order, holding a towel over his nose to soak up the blood. When we find nothing, a smirk of glee runs across his face behind the bloodied towel. It only lasts a brief moment. A glare from Smith cuts off any cheeky reply he might have been cooking up.

As we leave his apartment, Kingston is the most relaxed he's been since we arrived. He slams the door after us. Smith takes out another cigarette to smoke on the way down the street. By the time we get to the hearse, she has powered through the whole thing, and she puts it out on the pavement before getting in.

It's well after five now, and I've had about as much of this as I can take for one day. Once in the hearse, Smith brings the address for the final name up on the GPS. I decide to try to disarm this plan.

"Maybe we should call it a night and talk to the last one in the morning."

She pins me with a dagger-like gaze similar to the one she just gave our suspect on the way out of his apartment. I try to ignore it and continue my disarmament.

"These assholes are getting to both of us, Smith. We should sleep on it."

She continues to glare at me as she processes my words. I begin to wonder if I'm destined to have a broken nose after all. The pain from Atkin's blow has only recently subsided.

"Fine," Smith says.

Her brusque reply doesn't put me at ease. She looks away, and I start up the hearse and drive off. I wait a few minutes before I dare to ask, "Do you want me to take you home? I was thinking of clocking out with my transponder instead of going back to the department."

"Sure," Smith says, arms crossed tightly.

Her reply is the last of our conversation as I drive toward her apartment. All around us, the dark streets of Motor City loom hungrily. The light from the LEDs of billboards and street signs bathe the city in an eerie glow. When I pull up to the curb across from her apartment, Smith wastes little time exiting my vehicle. She's about to shut the door behind her when I quickly ask, "Hey, want me to pick you up the same time tomorrow?"

"No. Be later," she says firmly.

She slams the door and walks off toward her apartment. Despite her rudeness to my car and me, I wait to make sure she gets in safely, then drive off after clocking out with my transponder. I'm glad for the day to be at its end. It'll be nice to go home and spend a few hours talking to Rina and have some dinner. Maybe tomorrow's suspect will be our success story.

As I drive home, I think about all of our colorful encounters. There's the potential for Kelly, Kingston, and Atkin to file assault charges against us. If they try, only Kelly will have the weight for it to stick. There's nothing I can do either way. I decide to ignore the possibility of further troubles with them. There are more important things to focus on. Two days in, and we have nothing to tell us who killed May. Our most promising lead is proving to be a waste of our time thus far. Whoever we're looking for is dancing in Motor City's shadows as we fumble in the light.

CHAPTER 10

UNLIKELY AID

Honoring her request, I arrive at Smith's apartment building later than I did yesterday. I park the Cadillac and go up to the entrance. Before I have the chance to call up with the screen, Smith walks through the door and past me toward the car without so much as a "Good morning." I trail behind her, and we both get in. She brings up the information on our last suspect.

I decide to play along with her silence and leave for our destination. This lead takes us out past the edge of town to a small private property with a little house on it: one story, no more than a few hundred square feet. It appears to be from the late 1960s. I'm surprised to see it. Most of these kinds of places were torn down in the early 2030s to make room for urban growth. Its survival is no doubt due to its distance from the city. The resident of this aging relic is Janet Carter. I have a hunch this will be an interesting visit.

There's a chain link fence around the property's perimeter. I park on the street in front of it, and Smith and I get out. As we go through a small gate and up to the front door, I get a similar feeling to the one I had in front of Huxley's house, as if our every move is being watched.

I ring in on the screen by the door, since Smith seems to be uninterested in doing so. A young woman with a light brown complexion comes into view on the screen.

"What can I help you with?" she asks me.

"Janet Carter?" I ask. She nods. "We're detectives. Can we come in and have a word with you?"

"Badges," Carter says.

Smith and I pull out our badges and hold them up to the viewing screen. Carter studies them carefully, then says, "All right. Come in."

As the door opens, my heart sinks. Janet Carter is in a wheelchair. At best, we are about to take down a disabled woman for a crime; at worst, she isn't our suspect. I fear we're about to find ourselves at a dead end. We enter and follow Carter to a room filled with her equipment.

"Not sure why you're interested in me. No one hardly comes out here anymore," she says.

I sit in a chair near Carter. "Why's that?"

"I was the best hacker in town until I got mugged a few blocks over. The bastard shot me right through the spine. Nobody wants to hire a disabled woman. It's like they think I'm slow or something. But this shit"—Carter gestures at her wheelchair—"didn't affect my mind."

"So what do you do these days?" I ask.

"Just odd jobs. Whatever pays the bills. I'd love to make enough for the surgery to fix my spine. The bitch of it is anything that pays well enough isn't legal." She sighs. "But I guess my problems are beside the point. What can I help you two with?"

"I don't think you can," Smith says bluntly.

She makes as if to leave, but Carter says, "If you don't mind showing me what you have, I may be able to help you. It would be the most interesting thing I've done in a long time."

Smith pauses. I can see that she is weighing the possible gain from Carter's help against her frustration with the entire situation. After a moment, she pulls up a chair near mine and takes out her transponder to look up the footage. Once she has it, she sends it to Carter's server.

Carter opens the file and views it on one of her larger screens. There's silence in the room as we all watch it several times. Once Carter is content with what she's seen, she turns back to us and says, "I assume that we're looking at the odd movement of the flag?"

"Yes," Smith and I say, almost in unison.

"I imagine you've already figured out that it wouldn't take a lot of talent to do a hack like this. You probably also realized that the footage was spliced in from an earlier night at a similar, if not the same, time," Carter says.

Smith and I nod in agreement.

"I'm the last person you have info on, aren't I?" Carter asks, sounding disheartened.

"Yes," Smith says before I can make an excuse to hide the fact that Carter is our final suspect.

"I see. Well, this wasn't me."

"Is there anything else you can tell us about the footage?" I ask.

Carter ponders my question. Smith sighs deeply. I wonder if she's thinking back through the past few days. I'm sure she's as desperate as I am to find some piece of information to latch onto. Then Carter's eyes light up. "Deflection!"

"Huh?" I'm confused by her exclamation.

"If you were a real clever hacker and you were hired to do something like this, you'd be singled out immediately if it was perfect. What if the poor overlay of footage was intentional? It would suggest that the hacker wasn't as professional as they actually were. It would send the two of you on a wild goose chase," Carter says, proud of her theory.

Smith's eyes meet mine. It's clear we're having the same realization. She's already up and moving as I thank Carter for her help. She beams at me. I get the feeling it's the first time in a long time that she has felt so useful.

Smith and I waste no time piling into the hearse. I speed back into town, toward Jasper's apartment. The little shit has played us for fools. I find myself greatly anticipating his smug attitude being crushed by our discovery of his guilt. The Cadillac's tires squeal in protest around every corner. I fling the weight of the hulking hearse around fast enough that Smith grabs onto the armrest for some stability.

We arrive outside Jasper's shady apartment, and I screech to a halt. We get out fast enough that I almost forget to lock up. Smith doesn't bother to buzz him; instead, she flashes her badge across the screen to override it. The door clicks open, and we rush in and up the stairs, heading to his apartment as fast as we can without making too much of a commotion. At his door, both Smith and I draw our weapons. As she covers me, I flash my badge across the screen to his door to override its security. Only one of the many locks clicks open. I decide to give fair warning before using my revolver to blow apart the door.

"Jasper! It's the MCPD! Open the fucking door or I will!"

When there's no response, I take aim and fire. The massive rounds shatter the door into tiny pieces around the handle, and I kick it in with ease. Inside the apartment, the lights are off, screens flickering in the background. I find a nearby switch and flick it on using my elbow. I'm careful not to lower my gun.

Light floods the room, revealing a scene of devastation. There are screens and papers strewn across the floor, and pieces of broken equipment litter the already-cluttered room. Sprawled on the floor in front of his command center, Jasper is lying in a pool of blood. Smith finishes a quick sweep of the apartment as I holster my gun and go check on him. I find a weak pulse.

"Smith! Call it in. He still has a pulse," I shout.

She re-enters the room, her transponder already out. I take off my jacket and roll up my sleeves to look for the entry wound. I find it in Jasper's gut and rip a sleeve from my shirt to use to apply pressure to the gaping hole. It was already too late for my one nice shirt and tie anyway. Keeping Jasper alive long enough to tell us about his attacker could be our only chance to solve this case. *I hope the ambulance arrives quickly. I doubt he has long.*

The next few minutes take forever. When the paramedics finally arrive, they put on a proper bandage in place of my shirt sleeve. Smith and I help them carry Jasper out to the waiting ambulance. As they load him in, I ask one of the EMTs what his chances are. Her answer is as bleak as I expected.

"Looks like he's been in this condition for a while. I'm surprised he made it this far."

She closes the door, and the ambulance speeds off into the heart of Motor City. Smith and I are left standing there in the street. Blood covers my hands, and my jeans are soaked with it at the knees from me kneeling next to Jasper. We watch in dismay as the ambulance races out of sight. Our lead suspect is likely at death's door, and we're to blame for not seeing the truth sooner.

A crime scene unit arrives soon after the ambulance has gone. I carefully clean up and hand over my clothing to the CSIs after changing into some spare clothes I keep in the Cadillac. Changing on the street is awkward, but I use the back door of the hearse as a shield, and Smith holds the perimeter for me. As I finish changing, a call comes in on my transponder. Before I even answer, I know what I'm about to hear.

The words from the hospital's dispatch center ring out in my ear. I thank the automated assistant on the other end of the line, though there's little point in it. Smith looks at me expectantly. I crush our hopes as I shake my head. We put on sterile gloves, and I get some extra shoe covers out of the hearse before we go back up to Jasper's apartment. It's now the scene of his murder. I find myself thinking, on my way upstairs, how dark things are looking. *And it's only Wednesday.*

My boots, also covered in Jasper's blood, are in an evidence bag. I slip the shoe covers over my worn pair of black and white Converse before going into the apartment. Smith and I approach our initial search with similar levels of apathy, merely going through the motions. There doesn't seem to be much point in anything right now. I try to push through my disappointment enough to pay attention to the scene around us. We split up and rummage through the apartment for any possible clue.

Beyond the obvious damage caused by the attack that killed him, the apartment was a mess to begin with. Jasper was the type to have a one-track mind for his work. As with the scene of May's murder a few days before, there's a lot to look at but little that seems to matter to our case. It will take dozens of hours to go through Jasper's servers. After we've searched for a time, Smith and I converge in his small kitchen.

"You find anything meaningful?" The hope in my words sounds hollow. Smith shakes her head, confirming that we have little to go on. The kitchen is perhaps the messiest part of the whole apartment. Here, the Super K kiosk coffee cups are stacked in piles everywhere there's free space. I absentmindedly pick up one of the more recently used-looking cups to see what's inside. The smell of old coffee and rancid creamer assails me. I quickly close the lid and place it back on top of the stack. As I do this, I notice something, the only thing out of the ordinary I have seen so far. There's a small space on the industrial countertop that has been cleared for a drip coffee maker to sit on. The pot in it has had only one cup poured from it. I do a scan of the kitchen and don't see any mugs left out.

Without saying what's on my mind, I leave the kitchen, looking for any mug that could be lying around. Smith follows me, unsure what to make of my newfound enthusiasm. When I notice a mug perched on a shelf near Jasper's wall of now-destroyed computer screens, I proclaim my success.

"Yes!"

Smith's sharply raised eyebrows tell me she has no idea what I'm looking at so excitedly. "Have you lost it completely?" she asks, shaking her head.

I point at the coffee mug on the shelf. This does little to change the look on her face.

"He was a coffee drinker. So what?"

I carefully look into the mug without disturbing it. I'm further delighted to see that there's still black coffee in it. "This whole apartment is full of kiosk coffee cups. Not one mug in the kitchen has been used. And we have a pot of drip coffee that only has one cup missing. In this mug here is the coffee that was poured from the pot; there's no cream in it."

I can see Smith catch onto the idea. She takes a nearby kiosk cup and checks its contents.

"Yeah, you're right, Havoc. This one has cream in it too. I bet they all do except that mug you found," she says, smiling for the first time in a long while.

"Exactly. Our killer may well have been the one who drank from it."

Smith comes up beside me and takes a picture of the mug with her transponder; I take a picture as well. We'll make a note of it so the CSIs can analyze the cup for DNA or fingerprints.

"Well, we know one thing about our killer," I say with some optimism. "They take their coffee black."

Smith nods in agreement. We take a few minutes to examine more of the coffee cups to further prove our theory. We also check for any other mugs. I'm glad to find no evidence to contradict my hypothesis. Satisfied that we've found all we can for now, Smith and I head back downstairs. The CSI crew passes us on our way down, and I take the opportunity to inform them about the mug's importance. We also hand over our gloves and shoe covers.

Once we're back outside, we say our goodbyes to some of the other officers, then head back to the Cadillac. Smith and I pile in, and I start up the old V8. I take some time to appreciate the steady rumble of the engine. The sound calms my nerves. It's as if the deep tone of Elli's engine is saying *Relax*.

"We should probably head back to the station," I say reluctantly. "I get the feeling the chief is going to want to talk to me about this mess personally."

"Yeah. You're going to be on his shit list for sure. If you deal with him, I'll head over to records and see what I can dig up on Jasper," Smith says.

"Works for me. With any luck, I can join your efforts sooner rather than later."

I put the hearse in gear, and we roll off toward the department. I doubt our knowledge of how our killer drinks their coffee will provide Anderson any consolation on the matters at hand. I'll be lucky to leave his office with my job, let alone an ounce of appreciation for the last three days. We drive back in silent thought. I park the hearse in my spot, we both get out, and I lock up. Concentrating on these small moments of routine is providing me the only relief I can get this week.

On our way in, that thought sticks with me until we reach the point where we have to go in different directions.

"Good luck," Smith says.

Though I'm surprised by her encouraging statement, I reply in kind. "You too."

I make my way to the upper floor to see the chief. In a way, it's almost an honor to be seeing someone so high up twice in only a short time. It's too bad it has to be under such unpleasant circumstances. As before, the automated assistant directs me in. The only difference in its programmed response is the statement, "He is expecting you."

As I enter his stately office for the second time, Anderson is quite busy with the screen of his smart desk. He doesn't take the time to direct me to sit down, so I take the initiative and do it anyway. He continues with several tasks on the desk's touch screen for the next few minutes as I wait. When he's finished, he shuts the screen off and secures the room for our conversation.

"It's only your third day as lead detective, Havoc, and I am becoming extremely concerned," Anderson says without preamble.

"I understand, sir."

"Do you? To me, it seems more like you're just feeling around for something in the dark. Let me take the opportunity to turn on the light for you, Havoc. I expect better results than this. I took the liberty of looking over the suspects you and your partner have interviewed within the last few days. I'm finding it hard to understand why you spent so little time looking into them," Anderson says with a scowl.

"Jasper was our man. The others didn't have anything to do with May's death," I explain.

"Your confidence in that doesn't leave me feeling all that reassured, Havoc. A young woman in her prime is dead. Now your lead suspect is on a slab as well."

"Sir, if you're unhappy with my service, I'm sure Detective Smith would be more than happy to take lead. I believe she's more qualified than I am, sir."

"No shit, Havoc. However, she also happens to be Adrian Smith's daughter. No matter how qualified she may be, it would look bad if the press realized a mob boss's daughter was lead detective. That is precisely why I made you lead in the first place, Havoc. I get her brains and your heroic-looking face; now do you understand me?" Anderson's eyes are boring into me so hard he's practically staring into my soul.

"Yes, sir."

"Good. Now take another hard look at the people you interviewed. I don't want to take any more chances on this one. It would be even more embarrassing if you overlooked the killer in addition to letting your lead suspect get killed."

"Sir."

"That will be all, Havoc," Anderson says dismissively.

I quietly get up and leave his office. Thoughts sparked by his words swirl in my head as I take the elevator down to meet up with Smith. *There's something odd about Anderson being so determined that we take another look at the other hackers. I know in my gut that none of them had anything to do with this mess. It's almost as if he wants me to find something that might be there now. Something that wasn't there before.*

The thought that the chief could be mixed up in this seems like madness. But the way he referred to May as "a young woman in her prime" seemed … off. Something about it sounded almost personal. *This is still Motor City; strange and terrible things happen all the time,* I remind myself. *Crooked people spread like wildfire here.* I decide to let the thoughts simmer overnight and distract myself by helping Smith go through information on Jasper.

We find the expected long list of accusations, with only a few minor charges that stuck. The list of individuals that Jasper was rumored to work for is a veritable who's who of Motor City scum, also as predicted. Jasper scored high on an IQ test and stood out at the top of his class, graduating with a technology degree before he was eighteen. In a way, I find it a shame that such a brilliant mind was wasted so senselessly. Jasper's choice to pursue a life of crime with his talent was ultimately his end. I wonder what inspired him to go in this deadly direction.

Just as Smith and I are about to end our day, a message comes in on both our transponders simultaneously. There's no DNA or fingerprint evidence on the mug from Jasper's apartment. There is, however, evidence that it was wiped clean. Discouraged by yet another nail in our case's coffin, we clock out.

I decide to wait to mention my theories on Anderson until tomorrow. I can tell that Smith is as burned out as I am. It seems like the only way forward is to approach this with fresh minds. I drop Smith off at her apartment. She says a brief goodbye, and I watch her until she's safely inside. I can hardly wait to get home and take a shower. Jasper's dried blood is still all over me, which freaks out Rina until I reassure her that it isn't mine and briefly explain the day's events. Her consolation is to fix dinner while I take a shower. I try to ignore how the water runs off of me with a tinge of red. After my hot shower, I go downstairs and have a subdued meal with Rina.

I go to bed early, knowing I may not sleep well. The first few times I close my eyes, all I can see is Jasper's face. I feel sick to my stomach. Knowing that I might have been able to do something to stop his death is more distracting than my theory about Anderson. Eventually, I reason with myself that there wasn't much I could've done. This conclusion is enough to let my mind rest. I fall into an uneasy sleep, quicker than I had expected to. The toll on my body today was just as extensive as the toll on my mind.

I dream of my father's words about humanity. I dream of May and Jasper's faces. More disturbingly, I dream of Anderson standing over May and Jasper in the city morgue. A wicked grin crosses his face as he laughs at me. I wake up to the sound of wind howling at my window. It's still dark. The city is speaking to me again. She's laughing at me.

You failed again! Wanna-be!

As I eat breakfast with Rina, my thoughts from yesterday's meeting with the chief creep back into my mind. Combined with my disturbing dream, they take precedence over everything else. I need to decide if it makes sense to fill Smith in on my suspicions. It isn't so much that I'm concerned if she can be trusted; it's more a question of how insane the idea sounds.

Rina notices my distraction. "I know that look, Harvey. You're trying to decide if you should do something or not."

"You always know when something's on my mind, don't you?"

"It's sort of my job." She says this with a smile of triumph, savoring the satisfaction of yet again correctly guessing my thoughts. "Well, we don't have much time before both of us have to go. What's eating at you?"

I search for the words to use to reply without giving her too much information. I'm treading on dangerous ground with my suspicions. "I have a theory about the case my partner and I are on. I'm trying to decide if I should mention it to her or not."

"Not sure if you can trust her?" Rina asks, tilting her head.

"No, I think I can trust her. It's more that I'm not sure she'll believe me."

"That's easy, then. Just tell her. If it's what you believe, there's no reason not to tell her, if you trust her," Rina says, nodding sagely.

Her advice is as sound as any I could've hoped to hear. We finish our food quickly, then Rina walks off to the high-speed transit station, and I pile into Elli and go to pick up Smith. When I pull up in front of her apartment, I see her waiting for me on the front step. It would seem that I'm not the only one who's had trouble sleeping.

She spots the hearse and stands up. After she's inside, we drive off in silence. The steady hum of the V8 plays loudly in our ears. After a time, I decide to propose a stop for coffee. This is a twofold plan. First, I want coffee. Second, I've decided we should go somewhere quiet so we can talk. There's no better time to mention my theory than the present, but I need a safe location to share my hunch, somewhere far from the city's prying eyes and ears.

"You want coffee?" I ask.

"Sure," she says.

I head for the nearest Super K kiosk. Smith lights a cigarette and rolls down the window a crack so the smoke can escape. Both of us order coffee with sugar and cream. As the automated kiosk prepares our order, I enact the second part of my plan.

"After we get the coffee, do you mind if we go somewhere quiet to talk for a few minutes?"

The distance in her expression vanishes. "Sorry, I don't need more havoc in my life right now," she quips.

"Oh, come on! I mean, talk about the case."

"I don't think the coffee kiosk cares if we talk about the case in front of it," Smith says, curling her lip.

"I'm serious, Smith. There are too many ways someone could hear us in town."

"Fine. Where do you propose we go?" she asks, crossing her arms.

"The cemetery outside of town is quiet. No cameras within miles."

"Wow. Cheerful and dramatic. You must be a real hit with the ladies," Smith chuckles.

I glare at her. It's beyond frustrating to have to deal with her attitude on top of everything else. The kiosk makes an annoying buzzing sound to indicate that our coffee order is ready. I grab our drinks and hand her one. I lock eyes with her, and she finally gives a reasonable answer.

"Well, shit. If it's that important to you, Havoc, let's get it over with already."

The drive out to the old cemetery takes a while. We sip our coffee to pass the time, and eventually, Smith puts her feet up on the dash to stretch out a bit. There's little point in conversation yet; plus, I haven't figured out exactly what to say. The city begins to thin out as we get closer to our destination. Out here, the landscape is still much as it was before Motor City's great expansion. In the midst of the city, it's hard to forget the present. It surrounds you wherever you look, a constant reminder of our descent into the future. Out here, it's almost like going back in time. The hearse is like a time machine in her own way. I imagine that the old girl took regular trips out to this cemetery long ago; in those days, she would've been shiny and new. Normally, the world around her is more detached from the one she's passing through now.

Even though most things change over time, some don't. As we pull through the cemetery gate, there's a strange comfort in seeing all of the tombstones here to greet us. They remain almost untouched by the decades. The world outside the gate is modern, and twisted by man and machine, but here, everything is simple. Death has become a sobering comfort.

I drive in far enough that I know we won't be seen from the road, park alongside a stately row of old tombs, and shut down the hearse. I turn off all of the equipment on the dash as well as my transponder. When Smith sees me shut off my transponder, she says, "You really aren't joking around, are you?"

I don't bother to answer that, and she takes the hint and turns off her transponder as well. I switch on a hidden signal jammer under the seat to ensure our conversation's security.

"What did you just turn on?" Smith asks.

"Signal jammer."

"Right. I don't want to know how you got your hands on that. So, what's going on?"

I decide to get straight to the point. "After my meeting with the chief yesterday, I have the distinct impression that he's our killer."

She looks shocked. I can see her struggle to form a reply. "You're kidding, right?" she says, finally. "I practically held your hand through your first day. One meeting with the chief and you think he's our killer? You're fucking crazy."

"People keep telling me that. But what if I'm right? I'm almost sure he has something to do with these deaths," I say stubbornly.

"Why?"

"He brought up the idea a few times that we should take a second look at the other hackers. It's almost as if he expects us to find some new evidence that wasn't there before. And the way he talked about May didn't seem right; it was like he knew her," I explain.

"I think it's more likely he just wants us to be thorough," Smith says.

"I don't think that's it. It's ..." I struggle to convey what my intuition's been telling me. "It's the way he talked. Almost like he was nervous about something."

"Maybe he regrets his decision to make you lead detective."

"It's funny you should say that. There was another odd thing about our conversation. I told him that if he wasn't happy with me as lead, he should give you the position."

"What did he say to that?"

"He said I was right where he wanted me, a good face for the job. He told me he'd never make you lead, with your father being Adrian Smith and all. This way, he gets your brains and my face for the head of the department."

"Jesus, what a prick," Smith says, disgusted.

"Yeah, that's what I thought. On top of all that, he's given us some time to 'correct' our mistake in overlooking this so-called missed evidence. If there was no chance of him being involved in this mess, I can't see why he wouldn't have fired me on the spot. I think he needs us to provide a clean evidence trail against someone else."

"Holy shit, this is really fucked up. I can see why you wanted to come all the way out here to talk about it," Smith says.

"Yeah. What do you think we should do?"

She thinks for a second. "We have several friends and some family of Jasper's that we need to talk to. If we waste some time on that for the rest of today, we can maybe put off talking to the other hackers until tomorrow or Monday."

"Give Anderson time to sweat it out?" I nod. "That's a good plan. If he gets nervous enough, he might push too hard and make a mistake."

"Exactly. That's what we need him to do. Right now, all we have to go on is your intuition. We need something solid. An accusation like this one is tough to make stick, even with airtight evidence," Smith points out.

"Agreed. If you want to put their info into the GPS, we can get started."

She nods, and I turn off the signal jammer. We reboot our transponders, and I set up the GPS unit on the dash for Smith to use. After she adds the names and addresses, we make our way out of the cemetery to see our first name on today's list. I'm saddened to leave the cemetery's quiet comfort behind. Passing through its gate back into Motor City feels like we've entered an alternate dimension.

Cindy Dawson is the name of our first lead. Our records show that she's Jasper's on-and-off girlfriend. Her address is only a few blocks away from May's apartment. I park across the street and several cars down. Smith and I spot her lingering at the edge of the curb out in front of her house. Her skimpy outfit and avid interest in the occupants of passing cars indicate that she's looking for a "date."

I start to get out of the car, but Smith stops me by placing her hand on my shoulder. "Why don't you wait this one out?" she says softy.

"Why would I do that?"

"To me, you're just another cop. To a woman of color who happens to also be a sex worker in Motor City, you're a six-foot abominable white man with a handgun and a license to kill," Smith replies.

I catch a glimpse of myself in the rear-view mirror as she says this. I tend to forget that I'm not an average-size man; my scale matches that of my transportation. As does my color. I understand Smith's rationale.

"All right," I concede.

Smith gets out of the hearse, taking care to do so when Dawson will likely not notice which car she's coming from. I make myself less visible by slouching down in the seat, ensuring that the shadows in the Cadillac conceal me. I watch in silence as Smith makes her way across the street to interact with Dawson. She notices Smith and quickly turns to leave. Smith holds up her hands placatingly as she slowly walks toward Dawson. Somehow, she manages to convince Dawson to stop and talk with her. She offers Dawson a cigarette. This visibly calms Dawson, and she relaxes as she takes it. Their conversation continues for the next several minutes.

I wish I could hear what they're talking about, but the background noise of Motor City would make it impossible to hear them even if I was standing five feet away. Even trying to read their lips would be futile, assuming I knew how; from my perspective, Smith has her back to me. As they talk, all I can do is pay attention to the surroundings. There's a lot of foot traffic, and I kill some time trying to decide which of the pedestrians could be Techies. Cars drive past, a few newer ones and what looks like an ancient Volkswagen bug barely clinging to life. I hear what sounds like gunfire far off in the distance. All in all, this street seems to be entirely average for Motor City. Eventually, Smith turns away from Dawson and heads back toward me. As she gets into the car, I watch Dawson go back inside her building.

"What'd you find out?" I ask, impatient after having waited, useless, for the last five minutes.

"She didn't seem all that surprised to learn Jasper was dead," Smith says. "I guess in the last several months, he took on a few jobs that made her nervous. She said she hasn't seen him in a couple weeks."

"Did she have any idea who he might've been working for?"

"She knew he did some work for Adrian. Beyond that, she said, she didn't ask. I get the feeling that if she's heard any other names, she isn't about to share with us. I think hearing Jasper was killed kind of messed her up. She said she's going to go inside and lock her door behind her."

I think about this. "That would be wise indeed. I don't think it's safe right now for anyone who knew Jasper."

Smith nods. "Yeah. I told her if she has any friends out of town, now would be a good time to visit them."

"No shit."

I start up the Cadillac, and we head in the direction of the next name on the list. The morning drags on as we talk to several more of Jasper's friends and acquaintances. None of them has anything useful to say. We decide to give up on it for a while and head back to the department.

Smith gets us some lunch from the cafeteria while I check through the cases the other detectives are working on. I'm slightly jealous when I find out that most of them are progressing significantly faster than we are. Discouraged, I focus on eating my lunch, trying desperately to ignore my failure. All I have to go on is a questionable hunch and a half-drunk cup of black coffee with no fingerprints or DNA.

We head back out after lunch, this time to talk with some of Jasper's family. His sister is unconcerned by the news of her brother's death. She happily proclaims that she's glad not to have to deal with him ever again. On visiting his mother, we find just as little concern about the loss of her son. I get the distinct impression that Jasper's mother is too high to give a fuck about anything. Her answers to our questions are a little too eager. Smith and I are tempted to take her in on principle; however, our time could be better spent elsewhere. Best to leave her for the Narcotics Division.

By the time we track down Jasper's father, it's nearing the end of the day. The man's a total slob, fat, and hostile to the world. It's obvious where Jasper got his foul attitude. Halfway through our conversation, I have to hold Smith back from punching him out. Her enthusiasm for violence is concerning, to say the least, especially knowing how violent I can get when anger takes over. I'm starting to worry that much of our future as partners will be spent in the HR office filling out stacks of complaint forms. As with all the other suspects, we leave with nothing of use to go on.

I drive Smith back to her apartment. I can tell that both of us are at the end of our rope. Dropping her off brings the fourth day of my new job to an end. I drive home knowing that tomorrow, we'll have no choice but to go back and talk with the other hackers again. I dread this. I'm sure that there will be information or evidence planted on one or more of them. Who will Anderson choose to set up for his crimes? Will it be straight-laced Bill Huxley? Snot-nosed goody two-shoes Brandon Kelly? Or maybe down-and-out Doran Atkin is the chief's intended fall guy. I see little chance anything would stick to Janet Carter. No matter what the case may be, we'll soon be forced to act. There's little time left for Anderson to slip up before we find ourselves forced to arrest the wrong person.

Again, sleep comes uneasily. I toss and turn most of the night. I wake up a few times and find myself wishing that some sort of crisis would come up before morning, anything to delay us from having to take another look at the hackers. We just need a little more time for the chief to make a mistake. Any mistake will do. Otherwise, another one of Motor City's hackers is liable to find a new home at the morgue.

CHAPTER 12

ROAD TO AN ELDORADO

My transponder's obnoxious alert signal wakes me up with a start a full hour before my alarm is set to go off. A quick look at its screen tells me all I need to know. The alert is for two officers down. They didn't even make it to the hospital. My initial sorrow is overcome by a despicable sense of selfishness as I rush to leave the house. This is exactly the kind of distraction from our case that I was hoping for.

When I pull up to Smith's apartment, she's already at the curb, and she gets into the hearse so quickly that I don't even have to stop moving. I burn rubber getting to the scene. There are already dozens of squad cars and cops there. It's only a block away from the building where the drug bust went down.

I pull into an available space, and we both get out and walk rapidly, side by side, toward one of the street cops who has taken charge of the scene.

"What've we got?" Smith asks him.

The tattoo on the side of his head tells us that we're talking to Officer Ken Masters. The forlorn look on his face expresses the mixture of loss and confusion we are all feeling over the death of more of Motor City's finest. He makes eye contact with both of us before filling us in. "Officers Chase and Martinez responded to a tip that there was a drug deal going down on this corner. We got a call in from Chase about a half hour ago; said her partner was down and she was hit. Chase was still alive on our arrival. Martinez was DOA. Chase passed away en route to the hospital. We were notified a few minutes ago."

What a shitshow. "Are there any surveillance cameras in the vicinity?" I ask.

"We checked that, sir. The only one near this corner is busted," Masters says.

"Damn," I say. I find it distracting that he has referred to me as "sir."

I move past Masters, Smith at my side. I cringe when I see Martinez on the sidewalk. He's taken one gunshot to the face and two to the chest. His name tattooed on the side of his head is the only thing that makes him recognizable. The sobering image reminds me that our tattoos are the modern equivalent of dog tags. There's a deep red pattern stained into the sidewalk near his body. Drag marks through the blood indicate that this is where Chase was shot down. She made it several yards, her trail ending where the ambulance picked her up.

Officer Masters walks up behind us as we view the crime scene. "Did Chase say anything about their attacker?" Smith asks him.

"No, ma'am, I'm afraid not. You'd have to check with the EMTs to be sure, though."

Officer Masters' gaze darts to Martinez's body; then he turns and goes back to his watch. He's visibly shaken by the spectacle, holding his hand over his mouth and nose to avoid spilling his stomach contents. Smith and I spend the next several minutes scanning the area. The blood spatter suggests that there was only one assailant and that all shots were fired from the same direction, but only ballistics will tell for sure what happened here.

The crime scene crew shows up. They take several detailed photos of Martinez's body and the rest of the scene before they load him into a morgue van. By now, a crowd has gathered around the perimeter of the crime scene. By lunchtime, the city will be in an uproar. Cops die all too often in Motor City. Though people are quick to forget it each time it happens, it always stirs things up in the department. This helps make Motor City a rushing torrent of chaos as the cops end up on edge. A lot of Serenity officers will meet their quota tonight. Normally apathetic, officers throughout the city will be fueled by intense albeit short-lived rage.

Smith and I band together with several of the officers to canvass the neighborhood. By midmorning, we've busted a few drug dens and talked to dozens of potential witnesses. Unfortunately, by lunchtime, we're no further along than we were when we arrived. After a quick bite of lunch on the go, we meet up with Sergeant Mitchell. Chase and Martinez were Serenity Division, so ordinarily, Carson would have been in charge of things. Drugs take precedence, though. No doubt it was Anderson who asked Mitchell to step in today.

We give her a detailed description of the morning's events, then go with her in her SUV to meet with the families of the two deceased officers. Martinez leaves behind a wife and young child. Chase has a sister, as well as a boyfriend from the Serenity Division. Sergeant Mitchell does most of the talking. Smith and I take turns offering words of encouragement. Our consolations seem hollow. Words can scarcely make up for the loss of life.

Once we have informed the officers' friends and family, Mitchell gives a statement for the evening news. Smith and I stand back and to the side of the commotion of the news conference. I know all too well that there will likely be little justice for the two officers, but to keep up the department's image, many lofty goals and statements will be made today and into next week. However, once public interest drops, so will the chances of finding the officers' killers. At the end of the day, it'll be on the back burner of our case log. The only upside it has brought comes from its being a distraction. Our other case has had a whole day to simmer, not enough to shake anything new loose, but enough to get us to the weekend. We take care of some reports before leaving the department.

The car ride back to Smith's apartment is livened up only by rock station beats. When we reach her building, I shut the engine off, and the radio goes silent.

"Well, that day sucked," Smith says.

"Yeah. I hate seeing good officers die."

She nods sadly and starts to get out of the Cadillac. I speak up to stop her. "What year Eldorado do you have, again?"

At first, she seems confused by the question. Her car troubles are clearly the furthest thought from her mind. Then she makes the connection. "It's a 1970. Why?"

"I think I've got a starter that would fit it. Got it by accident a few years back."

Smith looks surprised. "What are you trying to say, Havoc?"

"If you tow your car over to my place tomorrow, we can put the starter in. Get you back on the road."

"You aren't worried I'm going to take your ride again, are you?" she smirks.

I smile at this. "You'd never do a thing like that, would you?"

"Never." Smith shakes her head.

"Should I pencil you in for tomorrow, then? It'd be a good time waster while we let our cases stew for the weekend."

"I tell you what, Havoc, I'll sleep on it. Let you know in the morning?"

"Sure."

I can tell she's as happy as I am to have ended our day with a conversation that has nothing to do with work. She gets out of the hearse and goes into her apartment. As usual, I wait to be sure she makes it in safe. This time, she looks back at me. I wave, and she waves back with a little smile.

I head for home, relieved that the workweek is over. Rina and I have a nice dinner and watch a couple of the old *Mad Max* movies. Rina jokingly suggests that I put a hidden explosive device in the Cadillac to emulate the film. While that would be diabolically hilarious, I point out that Elli is too important to risk for some would-be carjacker. Later, I clean up the garage in case Smith does decide to drop by in the morning. I make sure I know where the starter is and check to see that it's in good condition. I realize that I will miss picking her up in the mornings once I help her fix her car. It's been kind of a shitty week, but I go to bed knowing that at least I have a good albeit slightly crazy partner.

I take full advantage of my Saturday morning by sleeping past ten. I wake up thankful that I did not dream in the night, at least not that I remember. It's the first time since last weekend that I actually feel rested. Once up and dressed, I check my transponder to see if there are any missed calls or messages from Smith. There's nothing of the sort, so I head downstairs for some breakfast.

I discover that Rina is not at home. Likely she has gone to visit a friend, or perhaps even a boyfriend. There have been a few occasions in the last couple of months when she has left on a weekend without mentioning her destination. There was a time when I worried about her dating, but I've had to come to terms with the fact that she's no longer a kid.

Rather than making a big production out of breakfast, I eat a bowl of cereal. This doesn't take up much time, and I soon find myself bored. After checking my transponder again, I keep busy by further cleaning the garage. I park my hearse on the street so that there's a clear shot for the tow truck, should it arrive. These activities only take me to noon, and I again find myself bored. I read up on the other detectives' cases as a way to pass the time. This is almost as bad as doing nothing. The boredom eventually puts me into a trance, and I fall asleep on the couch around one thirty. My dreams take me back to when I first found Elli.

Straight out of the orphanage and prior to locating Rina, I was an eighteen-year-old with no place to go. One of the shitty factory jobs the state provided me with gave me just enough money to get either a lousy apartment or a cheap car. Given the mechanical skills I acquired in school, I was inclined to favor the idea of the independence that transportation could provide. While scrounging around at a salvage yard outside Motor City, I stumbled across the hearse. She had been dumped there after her funeral home was torn down. The yard manager was intent on scrapping her out for her valuable parts. I took a huge risk and spent almost everything I had to take her away from there. I called her Elli after the doll my sister had when we were kids. The old hearse became the only friend I had, a connection to the best parts of my life, my past.

I rented a small space at a trailer park outside the city. I lived in the hearse for almost two years before I found Rina again. I got us into school through state grants, and eventually we were able to get a meager apartment. Once I tested into the department, we got out of there and moved into the old house we inhabit now. It was a long road to get here, and Elli has been with me through some of the hardest miles of my journey.

The incessant beeping of what sounds like a large vehicle backing up outside the house wakes me up. I fumble with my transponder and discover that I've missed a message from Smith. I rush to the window. Sure enough, I see a tow truck backing into the driveway. Smith is helping direct its driver. On the deck of the truck rests a hulking maroon Cadillac Eldorado. I dash out to aid in the process, opening the garage door on my way.

"I wasn't sure if I should come, since you didn't answer my message," Smith calls out. "The tow truck driver already had it loaded, though, so I decided to risk coming over anyway."

"Sorry, dozed off on the couch."

"No worries. I'm later than I expected. It took a while to find a tow company that wasn't busy on a Saturday," Smith replies, shrugging.

It's a tight fit, getting the Eldorado unloaded onto my narrow driveway. Once it's halfway off the deck, Smith gets in to use gravity to our advantage for the last part. For a tense moment as the hefty car gains speed, I'm concerned that it will hit the garage, or possibly go through it and out the back wall. To my relief, Smith puts on the brakes just in time to avoid disaster.

The tow truck driver does a quick scan of Smith's license plate to charge her account automatically. Smith thanks the driver, an older, tough-looking woman with a patch on her jacket indicating that her name is Sue. Sue wishes us a hearty "Good luck!" before getting back into her truck and driving off.

I look over the 1970 Eldorado to see what I'm dealing with. As with my old Cadillac, certain things are showing their age. The chrome bumpers are tarnished and a little rusty. The body is fairly clean, though the paint is dull like Elli's and peeling around the edges. All in all, the Cadillac's condition is close to Elli's; it's just a little more worn.

"Where did you come by one this clean?" I ask my partner.

"I got it from the police impound. Some drug dealer owned it. When he got shot, it went to the impound lot. I got it for a steal of a deal. I've been doing small stuff to it since then to keep it going," Shay explains, looking over her car proudly.

"Nice. This is definitely has the best version of the Cadillac big block V8. The smaller 429 in mine has some notorious oiling issues. Not as much power, either."

"Let's see this starter," Smith says excitedly.

She follows me over to the workbench, and I show her the stock starter I found. We pop open the Eldorado's hood, and I double check to make sure we have the right starter. Once satisfied, I gather the necessary tools.

"You ever do much of your own maintenance on it?" I ask.

"I've done a couple oil changes and fixed a few flat tires," Smith replies.

"That's better than most people would do. If you're going to drive around something this old, it's always a good idea to know how to fix it."

"True, but I haven't had access to a garage to work in," Smith points out.

"Fair enough. I'm going to walk you through this, but I'll let you do the work."

"Sounds good."

I get out the floor jack and show Smith how to set it up. I also explain to her where to put the jack stands as a safety precaution. Once we have the car at a decent working level, I show her how to disconnect the battery before we get started. I take the under-car creeper off of the hanger on the wall and hand it to her, along with a 9/16 socket and ratchet.

"The worst part is going to be the weight of the starter," I warn. "Once you have the two mounting bolts mostly out, support it with one hand and take them out with the other. I recommend not having your face under it in case you slip."

Smith nods in agreement.

"Once it's off and hanging by the wires, I can hand you down some wrenches to remove the cable connections."

After my brief tutorial, Smith slides under the old car and gets started. Once she's settled, I pass her an LED work light. Then I watch from above the engine to offer help if she needs it. After some swearing, she gets the mounting bolts out. I pass her the wrenches for disconnecting the cables. She struggles with this for a few minutes, then successfully gets them off.

"Now what? This thing doesn't seem like it wants to come out of the space it fits in," Smith says, huffing in frustration.

"Just wiggle it around a bit. It'll drop out one way or the other," I advise.

More cussing occurs before I hear the sound of success. The starter exits the vehicle with a loud thud as it hits the concrete floor below. I'm afraid it may have fallen on Smith, but a quick duck to look under the car confirms that she's OK.

"For a second there, I thought you might've gotten hit with it," I admit.

"Nope. Almost. It missed me by an inch," Smith says. This is not terribly reassuring.

She rolls out from under the car with the starter in hand. We place it next to the new one on the workbench. They look to be an exact match. I pass her some disposable rags to clean the grease from her hands.

"So, why are you really doing this for me, Havoc?" she asks bluntly.

"So you don't try to steal my car again. Like Walt recommended," I say in a joking tone. From the look in her eyes, I realize she's being serious and quickly decide to elaborate on my first statement. "Honestly?"

"Yep."

"This city likes to take whatever chance it can to kill you. My first partner, when I was fresh on the job, got shot on the way home from work. He lived a few blocks away from the station and had a habit of walking home after he clocked out. One night, a stray bullet from a drive-by shooting went right through his head."

"Damn, that sucks," Smith says.

"Yeah, it really did. Even the toughest of us shouldn't walk the streets alone at night. Making sure you have a car is a good way to make sure I get to keep having you as a partner."

"Thanks, Harvey."

Her comment makes me smile. It's good to hear her call me by my first name.

Shay reverses the process and installs the new starter in about half the time it took her to take the old one off. She manages to do it with about half as much swearing, too. Once she has it all buttoned up underneath, we carefully lift the big car off of the jack stands, then remove them and lower it to the ground.

Her last step is to reconnect the battery in the opposite order from how she disconnected it. Once she's done with this, she takes out her keys and climbs in. To our delight, the 500 big block cranks over and roars to life on the first try. A big smile makes its way across her face. It's the first time since we met that I've seen her smile genuinely. Her whole face lights up. I grin widely in return.

Out of the corner of my eye, I notice Rina walking up the driveway, back from wherever she might have been. On seeing her, Shay shuts down the Cadillac and gets out. I introduce them, and Rina gives Shay a firm handshake.

"Nice to meet the woman watching out for my big brother," Rina says.

"He's a handful."

Both of them chuckle at this. I deflect by changing the subject. "You want to stick around for dinner?" I ask my partner.

"You already helped me with my car. You don't need to feed me too," Shay says.

"Can't let the mechanic leave on an empty stomach. You fixed it, I just watched."

"All right, you've convinced me," Shay says, smiling and shaking her head.

She turns her back to Rina and me to head toward the house. Rina mouths the words "She's cute" in my direction. "Shut up," I mouth back. The three of us go inside, and I close the garage door on the way. Shay follows us to the kitchen. I provide Shay and Rina with some sodas and go about making stir-fry, our Saturday night tradition.

We laugh and joke about our jobs and school. I think the occasion marks the first time that Rina and I have had a guest over just for the hell of it. The process of cooking and eating dinner helps take our minds off our day-to-day problems. After dinner, Rina goes to her room to study. Shay and I retire to the living room and plop down on two of the comfy chairs facing each other.

"You ever drink anything stiffer than a soda?" Shay asks curiously.

"Not really. I spend most of my paycheck on this house and the hearse. Not much left after that."

"You're an odd one, Harvey," Shay says, shaking her head at me. At least there's a smile this time.

"So they say."

Now might be my best chance to get to know the real Shay Smith, I decide. "So, what led you to become the ass-kicking detective you are today? If you don't mind my asking."

I can see her chewing on my question. I fear I've asked too much, gotten too personal, but to my relief, she responds in a pleasant tone.

"Well, you already know my father's deal. My mother was a fool to get in bed with a man like him. Almost cost her both of our lives. The drugs made my mother a degenerate and me a blue-haired freak. Adrian never apologized to me for what he did to my mother. He did pay to put me through school and keep a roof over my head, though. When I tested into the department, I was actually excited about it. I guess I thought it was the best way to get back at Adrian for all of his shitty mistakes."

"Wow, that's a lot. Why detective, though?"

"I'm sure you know the drill. I thought I could make a difference as an officer. But being a government-sanctioned killer made me feel like I was on Adrian's side of the law. I fought to get into Homicide so I could make a difference instead of causing more death like my father."

"Sounds noble to me."

"How about you, Harvey? What makes you tick?" Shay asks thoughtfully.

"Well, Rina and I had good parents, but they died when we were young. That put the two of us into the foster care system. I went to an orphanage, and Rina ended up in an abusive home. I latched onto education to drag myself back up. Had a few good teachers along the way who inspired me like my father did before he died. Coming to work for the department got me enough money to keep Rina and me stable."

"Damn." Shay's eyes are filled with sympathy.

"Yeah, when I say it all out loud like that, it kind of hurts," I admit. "I was afraid I wasn't smart enough to get out of the Serenity officer beat. Didn't want to risk losing the stability I had. That drug bust changed everything, though. I realized maybe I could get something better out of my life."

Having confessed all of this, I sigh deeply. Shay has tensed up again, as if something I said or did has bothered her.

"Did I say something?"

She sighs in turn and leans forward. "I feel like I should be honest with you, Harvey."

"Sure."

"You've been so nice to me. I think you deserve to know why I've been being such a bitch to you," Shay says, a look of shame coming over her face.

"You're not a bitch, you just clearly define how you feel."

I'm trying to be diplomatic, but Shay isn't having it. "No need to sugarcoat it. I've been a bitch," she says bluntly. "I wasn't mad at you for taking the job or being late on the first day. You've just been trying to learn the ropes. It wasn't your fault I got dressed in a hurry the other morning, either; sometimes I forget about what makes people feel awkward. There's another reason besides all that surface bullshit." Shay's hands are clasped tightly over her knees.

"What?"

"You knew Ryker Ramirez. You were partnered with him on the drug bust."

"I couldn't forget him. That kid saved my life."

Shay runs a hand through her hair. I can see that it takes every ounce of strength for her to get the words out. "Ryker was my half-brother."

Her words hit me like a sledgehammer. *No wonder she's been tense around me from the first day we met.* "Shit. I'm so sorry."

"It's OK. There's no good reason for me to blame you. It's nothing short of a miracle that you made it out alive like you did," Shay says, tears in her eyes.

"Still, I can see why you feel upset around me. It must be hard to understand why I survived and he didn't. I don't know what I would do if anything happened to Rina. She's all the family I have."

"I think what my brother told me at the end is really why I've changed my mind about you," Shay admits. "He lived for a few days after the explosion. He was thrown clear of the building, but the fall broke his back. Both of us knew he was going to die. Toward the end, he made me help him sign a form to donate his lungs to you. I couldn't figure out why he would do that for someone he had just met. He said, 'Harvey's a good cop, and I won't be needing them anyway.' Bravest kid I ever met." Shay wipes the tears from her cheeks with the back of her hand.

"Wow. I don't know what to say."

As her words sink in, I understand why my sighing set her off when we were in the car a few days ago. I'm literally all she has left of the only family she cared about.

"I guess at first I assumed that most people are shitty," Shay continues. "I figured he was wrong about you. I figured you didn't deserve to have a chance he didn't get. But he was right, Harvey, you're a good cop. A decent man, too. I was wrong to treat you the way I did."

"You have every right to be angry that life isn't fair. Thanks for trusting me enough to tell me the truth," I say.

"Sure, Harvey."

"Ryker was a brave young man. It's a shame we lost him."

"I'll toast to that," Shay says, her eyes starting to dry.

She raises her soda can to me, and I clink my can against hers. "To your brother. A great man," I proclaim, and we drink to Ryker Ramirez.

Shay pulls out her transponder to check the time. "Shit. It's getting late. I should head back."

I check the time on mine as well. It's a little after ten. "If you want to, you can crash in our spare room tonight," I offer.

"Nah, that's fine. You've done enough for one day."

"Come on, I insist. Besides, it's bad luck to go driving off at night when you just did a car repair."

I can see the concentration in her eyes as she considers my offer. After some pondering, she says, "OK, fine, Harvey. But I owe you one for all of this generosity."

"Deal."

I hold out my hand and shake hers firmly. We get up from our chairs, and I go to get some sheets for the bed in the spare room. Shay follows me and leans against the wall as I dig through the linen closet.

"How can you afford a big house like this, anyway?" she asks, looking around the long hall.

"I get a sweet discount because I keep the old place in good working order. Most weekends, I end up playing carpenter or plumber."

"Nice," Shay says.

I show her to the guest room and tell her there's a bathroom down the hall and on the right.

"Thanks again, Harvey. I really mean it," she says.

"Don't mention it. Goodnight."

Shay closes her door, and I go down to the other end of the hall to check on Rina. After knocking on the door, I go in to find her studying with her wall screen.

"Shay's going to stay the night," I announce.

"Oh, really?" Rina says, eyes wide.

"In the guest room, Rina."

"Too bad," she replies, shaking her head.

"I'm going to bed. See you in the morning." I say, rolling my eyes.

I go downstairs and carefully back the hearse into the driveway in front of the garage. This is the first time in a long time that I haven't parked Elli in the garage at night. I head back upstairs and get ready for bed. Before I turn in, I hear the back door open. A glance out of my window confirms that Shay's having one more cigarette before bed. I wait until I hear her come back in before focusing on falling asleep. It's another force of habit; I can't rest unless the house is safe and secure.

To my surprise, sleep feels like it could actually come easily. This is one of the most relaxing days I've had in a long time. Learning the truth about Ryker was painful, but I feel better knowing how lucky I am to have known him. His sacrifice gave me a better life; his sister is making me a better detective. Sleeping in, working on cars, emotional growth, hanging out with my partner and my sister: How could a day in Motor City be any better than that?

"Thanks, man," I whisper into the darkness. I wonder if Ryker knew how much his selfless act would mean to me.

CHAPTER 13

UNLUCKY SUNDAY

I awaken a few minutes after nine, feeling well rested. I take my time getting dressed. For once, there's no reason to rush. When I get downstairs, I find Rina rummaging around the kitchen for breakfast. Disappointingly, there's no sign of Shay.

"Shay up yet?"

"Yeah, up and out, actually," Rina replies, turning her attention away from her quest for food.

"Oh. Did she mention where she went?" I ask, trying to convey casual interest.

"Yep. She told me to tell you she was going over to the crime scene from Friday. Said there was something she thought you two might've missed."

"When was this?"

"She left about twenty minutes ago. Said she'd be there a while if you wanted to join her," Rina says, getting herself some cereal.

"Right. I think I will."

I start to leave the house, but Rina stops me. "You might need these." She's holding out my car keys. "I had to move your car for Shay to get out."

I take them from her. "Thanks."

I grab my jacket and go out to the hearse, start her up, and head for Friday's crime scene. I'm curious what Shay might have come up with. The odds of finding anything that will point to

Chase and Martinez's killer seem so miniscule. I imagine that whatever she's found will make me feel foolish for missing it. I wish I had her powers of perception. I turn up the radio to catch a PBX single that I recognize.

As I reach the crime scene, I notice Shay's Eldorado parked on the street. When I see that the driver's door is slightly ajar, my mood changes in a flash. I screech to a halt and back into a space on the other side of the street, then jump out and scan the area. The sky is cloudy. The streets between the tall buildings are just bright enough for me to make out my surroundings. The most disturbing thing is the lack of background noise; I don't hear anything or anyone. In this city, that can only mean one thing: Something is wrong.

As my eyes travel to the spot where Chase and Martinez were killed, my concern turns into fear. Someone is sprawled out on the sidewalk. I grab the medical kit from behind the seat of the Cadillac. I move as fast as my feet can carry me and quickly get close enough to the body to confirm that my overwhelming despair is justified. Shay is lying on her back on the concrete, and beneath her, the broken sidewalk is rapidly turning red. The city hisses wickedly in my ear.

You fucked up again, wanna-be!

I can't listen; I won't.

One bullet has grazed the left side of Shay's neck, tearing her skin jaggedly. There are at least two more bullet wounds to her chest. I'm relieved and surprised to hear labored breathing. This must have happened just before I got here. I take a painkiller injection from the kit and administer it to her arm, then take out a few thick bandages and apply them to her chest wounds with one hand. I hold another bandage against her neck wound with my other hand. Firm pressure will help to slow the bleeding. I call out to my transponder, as I cannot risk taking my hands from her wounds.

"Alert! Officer down! I need immediate medical attention at our location! This is Detective Havoc. Detective Smith is critically injured."

The transponder plays three clear beeps from my jacket pocket, indicating that it has heard my plea. Shay's eyes flicker open on hearing my voice. Her lips quiver. She raises her hand and clamps it tightly on my arm. The bandages I'm pressing against her chest seem to be holding up, but the one on her neck is already soaked through.

The bullet must've nicked an artery. If I cannot stop the bleeding, Shay will likely perish before help arrives. I decide to risk it, moving my left hand from her chest wounds to replace my right hand on her neck. Her face contorts, and her grip on my arm tightens like a vise. I take out my revolver with my right hand and aim at a nearby brick wall. I brace myself as well as I can to combat the recoil and fire all five rounds in rapid succession.

"I'm sorry. This will hurt."

Her eyes widen at my warning. I remove my hand and the bandage from her neck and press the side of the barrel firmly against her wound, feeling her nails dig through my jacket sleeve. The smell of burning flesh fills my nostrils. Her mouth gapes open, but only a hoarse cry escapes her lips as she writhes in pain.

After a few agonizing seconds, I put my gun down and replace it with my hand and a fresh bandage.

Her grip loosens slightly. I change the bandages on her chest and reapply pressure to them with my left hand. Her lips quiver again. I try to dissuade her from speaking.

"It's OK. Help is coming. We can talk later. You should save your strength."

The blue in her eyes is afire. I cannot stop her from speaking. Her words come out broken up, an alarming amount of blood trailing from the corner of her lips.

"It … was … uh … Ander … son."

"I know."

She rests for a moment, her chest rising and falling rapidly. I hear air escaping from her chest wounds. One of the bullets must've pierced a lung. She grips my arm tighter as she speaks again.

"Car …"

All of the muscles in her face are tense, her teeth clenched tightly. I again try to quiet her.

"Don't worry about it now. We'll talk after they fix you up."

She nods, and we wait for the ambulance to arrive. Her wounds terrify me. Dozens of times, I've seen officers die from lesser injuries. I'm astounded by her strength of will. The wait for help is agonizingly long. Thankfully, her grip on my arm does not loosen. When I hear the ambulance sirens approaching, it's the most beautiful sound I've ever heard. After a minute more, the ambulance pulls around the corner and screeches to a halt near the curb beside us.

I don't move from Shay's side as the EMTs surround us and bring a stretcher. After quickly assessing the situation, the female paramedic helps me switch out the blood-soaked bandages for fresh ones. When we change to the thicker bandages, I'm relieved to see that the wound on Shay's neck isn't bleeding much. With Shay's wounds better managed, the paramedic takes over applying pressure to them as her partner helps me lift Shay slowly onto the stretcher.

We wheel her over to the ambulance, and I help them load her in. It's no small miracle that she has lasted this long. All I can do now is pray that she makes it to the department hospital. Other officers are arriving as I close the ambulance doors. I pay no attention to them. I make for my Cadillac to help clear a path for the ambulance.

I gently kick the door to Shay's Eldorado closed on my way by. I dive into the hearse and turn on the siren and the hidden flashing lights. I burn rubber on every corner and peg the needle of the speedometer as high as I can. Shay's ambulance stays hot on my trail. Cars honk their horns and brakes squeal around us; a few near misses mean little to me. Getting Shay help is the only thing that matters. It might be the only thing that's ever mattered.

At the hospital, I bring the old Cadillac to rest with the wailing sound of screeching brakes. I rush out and help the paramedics wheel Shay into the emergency room. I'm relieved to see that her eyes are open. Her teeth are still clenched tightly. As we roll through the ER entrance, I hear the scanner check my bar code tattoo. One of the EMTs uses a handheld scanner to clear Shay. Only officers are permitted in the department hospital. Civilians require prior clearance.

As we roll Shay into an operating room, I see a familiar face. Dr. Arnold raises his eyebrows and smiles reassuringly as our eyes meet.

"Havoc, give me a few minutes with her. Wait here," Arnold says. His confident tone calms me slightly.

He points to a bench in the hall right outside the room. I nod and take a load off as he goes in. With the click of the door closing behind him, the chaos stops. For the first time, I notice the blood saturating my hands and shirt. At first, I'm paralyzed by the adrenalin coursing through my veins. Then I try forcing myself to stand, but I'm unable to achieve anything but the violent convulsion of my limbs. Eventually, I bite my tongue hard enough that the pain pulls me out of it. My body feels heavy as I walk to the bathroom at the end of the hall.

Washing my hands and emptying my bladder provides some relief. I go back to the bench to wait for word from Dr. Arnold. My hands are still shaking. I clench them together in an attempt to make it stop. After a few minutes that take hours to pass, the doctor emerges into the hall.

"She's stabilized for now," he tells me. Relief washes over me so powerfully that it makes me lightheaded. "I'm curious, what did you do to cauterize her neck wound, Havoc?" Arnold asks, intrigued.

"I fired all the rounds in my revolver and used the barrel."

"That was a brilliant idea. If you hadn't done that, I wouldn't have the chance to help her now."

"Will she pull through?" I ask, hoping against the terrible odds.

"She has a fighting chance, thanks to you. I'll know more after surgery," Arnold replies.

I spot Walt rushing down the hall toward us. Arnold and I exchange a nod, and he returns to Shay's room. Walt comes to a halt near me. There's sweat on his brow and fear in his normally calm eyes.

"I just got the news on my transponder. What the hell happened?" he asks, trying to catch his breath.

"I don't know," I say miserably. "She went back to the crime scene where those two cops got killed on Friday. I went over to check on her and found her like this."

"Jesus. How bad is she?" Walt's eyes are wide.

"She took two to the chest, and the one that grazed her neck would've killed her if I hadn't shown up."

"Thank God for you, Havoc. What did the doc say?" Walt asks, relaxing a little.

"Says she has a fighting chance." I pause to think. "Can you do me a favor?"

"Sure."

"I'm going to give my little sister clearance to come stay with Shay. Can you watch out for both of them for me?"

"Sure thing, Havoc. What're you going to do?"

"Put an end to whoever did this."

The concern has returned to his face, but he nods slowly and then puts out his hand. Our handshake is firm but brief. I leave him there in the hall and make my way to the nearest exit. It is high time I have a discussion with Anderson. On my way, I send Rina a message with my transponder. If she takes the high-speed transit, she will likely be here soon after Shay goes into surgery.

As I leave the building, my gaze falls on an unwelcome sight. On recognizing me, Adrian rushes in my direction. His fists are tightly clenched, his eyes fierce. I imagine that the fact I have his daughter's blood all over me only heightens his anger.

"It hasn't even been one fucking week! You let my daughter get shot!" Adrian yells.

He's almost on top of me now, but I make no move to avoid him. I have no time for his anger. Mine takes precedence. I let him clench the collar of my jacket.

"I told you to watch out for her, you little shit!"

As the spittle from his words hits my face, his voice rings in my ears. I remain calm. His attack has provided me with a distraction that I desperately need. My hands stop shaking. My anger has taken over so completely that it's manifesting as a zenlike calmness.

"Well? Explain, Havoc!"

When I speak, I feel as if I'm watching myself from a distance. "I recommend you take your hands off of me, Adrian. Remember where you are."

"I don't fucking care! We're talking about my daughter!" Adrian shouts.

I remain composed, knowing that several officers will be here any moment. Besides, I need to save my anger for more deserving parties. Adrian is merely helping me cultivate it. "I'm the only reason your daughter is alive. I was there when she needed me. I want to find the asshole who did this to her as bad as you do, Adrian. Right now, you're making it difficult for me to do that. Back off, or I'll make you."

I see the same fire in his eyes that I've seen in Shay's. His teeth are clenched, and he makes a deep growling noise in the back of his throat, not unlike a dog ready to bite. Several officers burst through the door of the police department across the street and run toward us. Releasing all the air from his chest, Adrian lets go of my collar. The officers surround him, and one of them asks, "Detective Havoc, is there a problem here, sir?," her eyes darting back and forth between Adrian and me.

She and the other officers are holding their weapons on Adrian. He doesn't move, his glare still fixed on me.

"No problem," I say. "I would like you to take Mr. Smith to see his daughter."

"Sir?" she asks, surprised.

"You heard me. I'm giving Adrian Smith permission to see his daughter. Be sure that you stay with him. Escort him out if my partner wakes up and doesn't want him to stay."

She nods and places a hand on Adrian's shoulder.

"You have twenty-four hours, Havoc, then I take care of this my way," Adrian says, pointing a finger at my face.

"I'll take care of it before the end of the day," I vow. "Adrian, go see your daughter."

He reluctantly accompanies the officer past me and into the department hospital. As the other officers disperse, I go across the street to the department. I rush through the doors, giving the scanner barely enough time to recognize me as I pass. I make my way quickly to the elevators, almost knocking over an officer as I pass her. On my way up, I send a message to Walt letting him know that I've cleared Adrian to see Shay.

On the top floor, I walk right past the automated assistant. I ignore its passive protest, fling open the door to the chief's office, and march straight in. Anderson is behind his desk, and my old sergeant, Carson, is seated across from him. Carson turns as I enter. His eyes are bloodshot, the lids drooping. He hasn't shaven in a few days. I'm not the only one who's had a rough week. Chase and Martinez were Carson's officers. *He must feel horrible about losing them.* My anger cools slightly as I consider how irrationally I'm behaving. *The world doesn't revolve around me.*

Without looking my way, Anderson finishes their conversation. "That will be all for now, Carson."

Carson turns back to look at Anderson and nods, then gets up from the chair and passes by me. Briefly, he places his hand on my shoulder before leaving. The door clicks closed behind him. I'm alone with Anderson. My anger rises again. Moving toward the desk, I feel as if I've stepped out of my own skin. The Harvey moving toward Anderson isn't rational; he isn't calm. This Harvey is looking for blood, and he will have it at any cost. The city calls to me again, a howling wind outside Anderson's high windows.

Kill him! You can do it here, now!

I'm considering it.

"Sit down, Havoc," he says.

As I take a seat, I notice a cup of black coffee on the smart desk near Anderson's folded hands. This makes the skin on the back of my neck crawl. I think seriously about jumping across the desk and having at the bastard's throat. *It would be so easy to finish him off now, when he's vulnerable. And why not?*

God, what's come over me? My fists clench on the arms of the chair, my heart racing.

"I am thoroughly disappointed in you, Havoc. On Wednesday, I told you to look back into those hackers. Your failure to obey a direct order may well be what got your partner shot this morning."

The chief's words cause my teeth to clench so tightly I fear they will shatter. It's all I can do to keep my emotions from exploding out in violence.

"Since you didn't bother to look into them, I did," he continues. "Turns out, as I suspected, one of the hackers fits as our killer. Janet Carter."

"Janet? She's in a goddamn wheelchair!" I almost yell, trying to hold back my rage.

"That may be, but the woman is a con artist and a hacker, Havoc. If you would have bothered to look into your suspects properly, you would have found the records stating that her spinal injury was healed. That isn't the only thing we found on her, either."

As my emotions swirl, Anderson brings up Janet's file on the smart desk. He shifts the screen so I can read it. After I scan the information, my grip on the chair loosens. Not only is Janet able to walk, but there's also a restraining order against her, filed by Jasper. I've neglected the first rule of my own code: Never substitute emotion for fact. But this is all easily fabricated information, and it's not enough to overshadow my hatred for Anderson. It doesn't curb the gut feeling that he's to blame.

"It's suspicious, I'll give you that," I admit. "But this alone isn't enough to place the blame on Janet."

"Then maybe this will convince you. This footage was taken from a camera a few streets over from where your partner was shot this morning."

Anderson pulls up a feed from a file folder on his desktop, flipping the screen with the flick of his wrist so that I can see it. I watch the feed play out in a state of disbelief. The grainy image of Janet Carter walks around the corner of a building. I recognize the street as one near where Shay was shot. Clearly visible in her hand is a 9mm pistol. There's also a chilling look of intent in her eyes as she passes the camera.

As if this isn't enough to set my thoughts afire, Anderson brings up a second feed from a few minutes later. This one shows Janet running away from the scene, gun still in hand. She glances back briefly, revealing blood spatter on her cheek. Everything washes away, and Anderson's words come to me as if I'm under water.

"The department has lost two good officers this week, Havoc. I'm afraid we may lose another before the day is out. This is your last opportunity to fix this. Bring Janet in. Finish this thing right, or I will."

His words rattle around in my mind, but they're overshadowed by my newfound hatred for Janet. I cannot seem to force myself to respond. I stand up; my body feels heavy again. Shay's blood still covers my clothes. There's only one way to solve this mess, to get even. *Janet must pay.*

"Yes, sir."

Without another word, I go out into the hall and back downstairs. I leave the department and go across the street to the hospital, my feet carrying me as if I'm on tracks. There's no time to check in on Shay. Taking down Janet is the only thing that matters now, the only thing that will satisfy the gnawing hate. As I speed off in the Cadillac, a sliver of humanity breaks through my anger. I call Walt from my transponder, and he answers immediately. There's a decidedly concerned tone to his voice.

"Harvey, where the hell did you go?"

"I have to finish this. Let me know how Shay does."

I end the call before he can respond, flicking on my lights and siren to get through traffic faster. How could I have been so blind? Janet was playing us from the start. I can hardly believe I allowed myself to blame the chief. *It's strange that she chose to kill May, but maybe it was jealousy. Perhaps this was some fucked-up love triangle, Janet at its pinnacle. Or maybe Jasper was the one who killed May. That would make more sense. May and Janet might have been friends, and Janet could've killed Jasper out of anger. But what of Chase and Martinez? Were their deaths part of this mess? And what of Shay's words? She said it was Anderson. Wait … what if she was trying to say it* wasn't *Anderson? Her ability to speak was impaired by her neck wound.*

These thoughts quickly fall away. In the grand scheme of things, it doesn't matter. Talking with Janet will provide answers. Killing her might even provide enough satisfaction to relieve the hate in me. I reach Janet's house in half the time it took us to get here before, skidding to a halt in front of her chain link gate. I carefully reload my revolver after realizing I haven't done so since firing off the rounds earlier, then get out of the hearse. I don't bother to lock up; there's no time for it. I walk with long strides up to Janet's front door. Once again, a terrifying calm has come over me. I let the wind carry the city's wisdom to my ears.

Kill her!

"OK."

Who said that? Was it really my voice that agreed to such a heinous idea? I press the call button. After a moment, Janet's face appears on the screen.

"Havoc? Long time no see."

Trying to hide my anger behind what I can only assume looks like the smile of a deranged man, I ask, "Can I come in and talk a minute?"

"Sure," Janet says, apparently not noticing anything amiss.

The door clicks open, and I go inside. When it closes behind me, I don't have to force the next action. The logical side of me is screaming at me, but breaking my code comes more easily than I care to admit. Janet's eyes widen. Her hands grip the arms of the wheelchair as I pull out my revolver and aim it squarely at her face.

"Stand up, bitch!"

I feel like a child watching myself helplessly from a small crack in a closet door.

"I can't! You know I can't!" Janet cries out.

"If you make me ask again, I'll kill you on principle."

The only sound in the room is that of our rapid breathing. I'm alarmed at how far I have let myself go, but I cannot stop it. I've gone too far to turn back. Janet grips the arms of her wheelchair tighter and hoists herself up from it. Once on her feet, she kicks it backward with one foot and raises her hands above her head.

"Now you get to explain to me why you killed Jasper," I say. "Was it because he killed May? No, fuck them; why did you try to kill my partner this morning?"

I click off the safety to underscore the importance of my words. The gun's barrel is only inches from Janet's face. *Harvey, what are you doing? Where's your humanity?* I trap my logic inside and push past it.

"I didn't do any of those things, Havoc," Janet says, shaking uncontrollably.

"Try again."

As I fire past her head, she flinches and ducks to one side. "Shit! I swear I didn't do it, Harvey!" she pleads.

"Then explain the fucking wheelchair!" I shout. "And what about the restraining order Jasper filed against you? And how about the goddamn footage of you in the neighborhood where my partner was shot?"

"The wheelchair is a gimmick. It makes people feel sorry for me, all right? I use it because it makes it easier to get work. The restraining order was from years ago. Jasper filed it to screw with me after we broke it off. I don't know why there's footage of me in her neighborhood, but it wasn't me," Janet says in a rush, practically babbling.

"Prove it."

"I can't. If you want to blame me, there's nothing I can do to stop you," Janet says.

I close my eyes and try to focus on my breathing. With my nerves eased slightly, I ponder what Janet has said. Am I looking at the killer? Or has Anderson given me another clever diversion to keep me from the truth? Janet would make for a convincing suspect because she's a liar and a con artist. But the fear in her eyes and the shaking of her body could indicate her innocence. There's little tangible evidence to support either reality. I decide to use the only evidence I have for sure. It's thin, but it's all I have to go on besides my wavering emotions.

"How do you take your coffee?"

"What?" Janet asks, now as confused as she is scared.

"You heard me."

"Ah … cream, no sugar."

I lower my gun, and Janet lowers her arms. Thankfully, my anger ebbs, and I regain control of myself. The compulsion to unload my gun into her fearful face has subsided.

"How come the way I take my coffee just kept you from killing me?" Janet asks, sinking backward into her wheelchair.

"The only thing I know for sure at this point is that whoever killed Jasper drank their coffee black."

"That isn't much to go on. What happened to your partner?" Janet asks, trying to catch her breath.

"Shay got shot this morning," I say grimly. "She's in surgery now."

"That sucks." She looks genuinely sorry. "Do you have any suspects besides me?"

"One. It's worse than you could imagine."

"Sounds like I'm safer not knowing," Janet says as she wipes the sweat from her forehead.

"If I'm right this time, no one's safe. Do you have a car?"

"Ah … no. But I could borrow one from a friend around the corner."

"That's even better." I regard her for a moment. She's not a bad sort, despite everything. "You need to disappear."

"What are you going to do?"

Her words seem distant to me. I force myself to respond.

"For now, I'll pretend I didn't meet up with you. It's going to take a miracle to find evidence against the real killer."

Janet doesn't move. Sweat is pouring off her forehead, and she's still shaking. Neither of us could've known this would be the way our day would turn out when we woke up this morning. For the next part of this journey, I need to be alone. If Janet remains in the picture, she'll be a liability.

"Go, now!" I bark at her.

This stirs her into action. She rises and brushes past me into the kitchen across the hall. A minute later, she passes me again, a set of keys in her hand, and leaves without another word. I go to a nearby window and watch her as she makes her way around the corner. She's half walking, half running—probably running from me more than anything else. Soon after Janet disappears from sight, I hear a car come to life in the distance.

I drop into a nearby chair, unable to hold myself upright any longer, and weigh my options. The situation I'm facing is more than just challenging; it's impossible. Anderson has to be behind all of this, but I don't have any more proof of that now than I ever have. Shay is the only witness, which puts her in grave danger if she pulls through surgery.

If I call in to dispatch, Janet's house will be crawling with cops within minutes. I have to give her time to get out of town. There's no reason to trust anyone besides Shay and Walt. If Anderson's the one behind this, who knows how many cops are in his pocket? The only one I can think to call is Sergeant Carson. I decide it's worth a shot. The call rings through several times; then, unfortunately, it goes to voicemail.

"Carson, it's Havoc. I can't explain over this line, but I could use your help. I'll send you an address. Come as quick as you can when you get this."

I send him my location, then take a moment to compose myself. Closing my eyes and breathing in and out deeply takes the edge off. All I can do now is wait. Everything is up in the air, and I have nowhere to turn. While I wait, I sort through the evidence in my head. Everything Anderson has said; the coffee on his desk and in Jasper's apartment. The fabricated footage against Janet, no doubt one of the tricks Anderson learned from Jasper. Shay's few words stand out. I mutter them to the empty room.

"It was Anderson."

CHAPTER 14

THE REAL MARK

The minutes tick by. I hear the sounds of the city rumbling in the background. It's carrying on as if nothing has changed. I've changed, though, sunken downward into its depths. Motor City doesn't care that my struggle almost caused me to kill an innocent woman. My brief and dangerous lapse in judgment almost turned me into the very evil I'm trying to fight. If I perish today, the city will still be here tomorrow to laugh over my gravestone. *I need to fix this. I have to make up for losing my grip on humanity.*

I wonder what will happen when the news hits. This shitstorm has the potential to tear the department apart, although maybe that isn't the worst outcome. The truth must come out; it doesn't matter what the cost may be. The truth could even help set this city free. Hell, maybe the truth can take away the burning shame coursing through my veins. It probably won't, though. That would be too easy.

I hear a vehicle pull up outside Janet's house. Carefully, I get up and peek through the yellowed curtains of her front window. I'm hoping that the sound signifies Carson's arrival. Instead, I see Anderson get out of one of the department's few new squad cars. I move back from the window, clicking off the safety of my gun, and aim at the door.

An alarm sounds, indicating that Anderson is overriding the door pad with a badge scan. He enters the room. When he sees me, his eyes narrow, but his hands remain at his sides.

"It's over, chief. I know the truth." I hold my gun steady, pointed at him.

"It is? On the contrary, Havoc, I think things are heating up."

A crooked grin makes its way across his face. His hand moves toward his sidearm. I fire one round, grazing him in the shoulder. He grits his teeth and takes aim at me. I duck, the bullet whistling past my head by a few inches. He charges at me, eyes wild, and we grapple. We both get a few more shots off but don't manage to hit each other. Breaking glass and splintering wood adding to the chaos of our struggle. Anderson manages to wrest the gun from my hand by gripping my wrist and firmly twisting it backward. I hear the sound of bone breaking. Pain floods into my hand and up my arm.

I fall to my knees, the pain crippling me. Anderson staggers back, brushing the hair from his face. He holds his gun to my head. There's nothing I can do. My gun is empty, and it fell from my limp hand as I collapsed to the floor.

"Well, shit, Havoc, that was exciting. Productive, too. Thanks to your half-assed shot, I have a good story to tell about how you attacked me," Anderson says, a wicked smile distorting his face.

"Why?"

I speak through clenched teeth, wondering what happened to all the blind hatred I had only a few minutes ago. *Why didn't I shoot him in the head instead of the shoulder? How the hell did I go from a stone-cold killer to a coward? I've failed everyone.*

"I worked myself to death for this city, Harvey. I started on the streets before it was mandatory to serve the department. I clawed my way to the top. I played by the book my whole life. I am not going to let one mistake ruin all the good I've done for Motor City. I can't," Anderson says, shaking his head firmly.

"How can you call killing people a mistake?"

"It was for the greater good, Harvey," he explains. "I cared for May. Killing her is my only true regret in all of this. All the time we shared together ruined by one bad night. It's unfortunate that she knew my secrets, regrettable that she made me angry. I can't afford to be selfish, though. This city needs me. It wouldn't survive without me." He sounds like he actually believes the bullshit he's saying.

"You're fucking insane, Anderson."

"I'm the only one thinking clearly, Harvey," he retorts. "Can't you see that? I tried so hard to give you an out. All you had to do was take down Janet Carter. We both could have walked out of this free and clear. Instead, I have to lose four good officers this week, not three."

His words seal my fate and Shay's. I close my eyes and prepare for the end. I hear the city's sinister whisper in my ear. *You're dead now, Harvey!*

The city's right. I concentrate on the pain in my wrist to distract me from what's coming. From behind me comes the faint shuffle of stealthy footsteps. *Is there someone else in the room?* Before I get the chance to look, a deafening shot rings out.

The pain I expected doesn't come. I open my eyes to see Anderson slump to the floor, blood oozing from a wound on his forehead. I whirl around. Carson's gun is raised, the barrel smoking.

"Holy shit, what did I do?" he says.

I'm not sure which of us is more shocked by what just happened. He lowers his weapon, absently puts it back in its holster, and holds out a hand to help me up. I'm amazed that none of the bullets from my gunfight with the chief managed to hit me. My face is beginning to swell from one of Anderson's harder blows.

"Seriously, Havoc, what the hell is going on?" Carson asks, taking out his vape to calm his nerves.

"It was Anderson." I echo Shay's words again, hardly able to stand, let alone speak, as the adrenalin rushes through me.

"What was?" Carson asks. To him, my words must be nonsense.

As I pull air into the lungs Ramirez gave me, emotions flood over me like a tidal wave. I force out a response to Carson's question.

"Anderson killed May. He took out Jasper to cover it up. I don't know why he killed officers Chase and Martinez, but somehow Shay realized he was behind that too. Anderson must've been keeping an eye on the crime scene. Maybe Shay saw him there. Then he would've had to shut her up."

My words take time to sink in. Finally, Carson says, "Goddamn, this is going to take a stack of paperwork to sort out. Please tell me you have evidence against him." A plume of vapor escapes his lips.

"Shay got a good look at him. She told me so when we were waiting for the ambulance. He tried to cover his tracks by faking footage against Janet Carter. This is her house."

"Let's hope Smith hangs in there for the sake of both our necks." Carson sighs.

"I'm just glad it wasn't me who shot him. I think you get the short end of the stick on this one, Carson."

He smiles and shakes his head. "Even after you leave my department, you still find a way to be a pain in my ass, Havoc." I manage to let out a dry laugh.

Carson calls it in on his transponder. I check in with Walt and find out that Shay made it through surgery. I tell Carson, and we each let out a deep sigh of relief. While we wait, for the sake of procedure, Carson checks Anderson's body to confirm that he's gone, though that head wound spelled instant death. He deserved far worse.

A few minutes later, what looks like the entire MCPD shows up. We remain at the scene for the next few hours. There are several statements both of us have to make. Eventually, Sergeant Mitchell arrives, and Carson and I go over everything we know one more time. She considers the information carefully as we speak, digesting our every word with her calm stare.

"This is one of the most disgusting breeches of justice I have seen in all my years. Motor City owes the two of you a great debt, if what you say is true," Mitchell says.

Carson and I nod in thanks.

"Until your partner wakes up, Havoc, I would ask that both you and Carson turn in all of your weapons. Go back to the department and stay there until I get back. I have to go appease the news crews outside," Mitchell says.

While she goes to speak for the cameras, Carson and I go out to our vehicles. I notice that he has parked his car a block away. His slick entry through the back of Janet's house is the only reason I'm still alive. I fire up the Cadillac and head across town to check on Shay. Driving is awkward and painful. I hold my broken wrist against my chest and drive with my left hand. I park the hearse in the garage and stagger over to the department hospital. I decide to check on Shay before tending to my own injuries. I find Dr. Arnold speaking with Walt and Rina in the hall. Rina runs up to wrap her arms around me.

I wince, trying to protect my wrist from her embrace. Her eyes are filled with concern and relief.

"Jesus, Harvey, are you OK?"

"Not really."

Dr. Arnold and Walt come over. When Rina releases me, Arnold's eyes dart to the hand I'm favoring. "May I take a look?" he asks.

I raise my hand shakily toward him. He holds it lightly as he checks my wrist with the tips of his fingers. Their warmth helps ease the pain a little.

"We should get that set right away," Arnold says, staring at me over the rim of his glasses.

"How's Shay doing?"

"She's doing well. Hopefully she'll wake up in the next few hours," Arnold says.

I start toward Shay's room, pulling my hand from his grip. I grit my teeth as a new wave of pain pulses through my arm.

"Hold on, Havoc. Shay can wait, your wrist can't."

Arnold's voice is firm but soothing. I heed his words and follow him to an empty room across the hall from Shay's. He has me get up on the table and prepares to set my broken wrist. After giving me a painkiller shot, he waits for it to set in, then works his magic. I watch my wrist bones slide back into place with a loud snap. The skin is beginning to swell and darken over the bone. Using a premade brace, Arnold tightly bandages my hand and arm so that the wrist will stay immobile, then gets a sling from one of the cabinets and helps me shift my arm into it without hurting myself further.

"There. Now you can go see your partner," Arnold says, nodding in approval.

"Thanks, doc."

Arnold goes to tend to his other patients, and I go into Shay's room. Walt and Rina are already there, sitting on a bench near her bed. On seeing the gentle rise and fall of her chest, I feel relief for the first time in a long time. I walk over to her bedside, noticing that her skin isn't as pale as it was this morning. Her eyes are closed, but her face is no longer clenched in pain. After thankfully watching her calm breathing for a while longer, I sit down next to Walt and Rina.

"What happened?" Walt asks.

"Chief Anderson was behind all of it. He murdered May and then killed Jasper to cover his tracks."

Rina looks at me with big eyes. Walt sighs heavily. "What about Chase and Martinez?"

"I'm not sure why he killed them. Shay figured it out somehow. She must've run into him at the crime scene or something. I don't know."

"What a fucking mess."

Walt's words surprise me. I haven't heard him swear like this before.

"No shit," Rina chimes in.

Well into the evening, Rina decides to go home. I give her the keys to the hearse and tell her I'm staying here all night. I'm so exhausted that I pass out cold with my head against the wall. At around ten, Walt wakes me up to let me know he's heading home.

Before he leaves, I ask him to bring me a blanket and some pillows. That way, I can crash more comfortably on the bench overnight. A short time later, he returns with my supplies. I thank him and tell him to get a good night's sleep. It takes a while to get into a decent position to rest. I'm trying not to jar my wrist. Seeing Shay's chest rise and fall methodically helps calm me. As I fall asleep, my last thought is how grateful I am for this day to be over.

I awaken around nine in the morning to bright light creeping through the curtains on the small window above Shay's bed. She still hasn't woken up. The wall screen across from her bed shows that her vitals are steady. I get up and raise my arms above my head, stretching. The pain in my wrist produces a dull heat.

I venture down the hall to take a leak. This process is more time consuming with my injury. I haven't felt this vulnerable since I woke up from my last hospital visit. I finish and wash my hand. It's the first time I've bothered to look at myself in the mirror since my fight with Anderson.

The bright white light from above the mirror amplifies the pain in my already throbbing head. My right eye is swollen, and there's a scrape across my cheek. I dampen my hand and run it through my hair, attempting to wrangle it into place. I splash cold water on my face and dry it with a few paper towels from the automated dispenser, then return to Shay's room.

She's the same as when I left. My stomach growls loudly when I sit back down. The lack of nourishment is surely contributing to my growing headache. I dare not leave Shay again, though. *I'll wait here with her until she wakes up.* There's plenty of time to eat later; everything else can wait until later. I bought time for us both. I even bought time for the city that tried so hard to kill me. I've fought too hard and come too far to leave my partner now.

CHAPTER 15

AIR OF CHANGE

The morning disappears as quickly as it came. Around noon, Rina messages me for an update, and I tell her that everything is the same as last night. My stomach's growling grows more aggressive as noon passes into one, then two. I give up focusing on the vital signs screen after a time and let my thoughts travel to the case. It doesn't help my head, but it does help distract me from my hunger.

Everything fits perfectly except for Chase and Martinez's deaths. *Why did Anderson decide to kill them? What did Shay go back to the crime scene hoping to find?* I don't like the feeling that I'm missing something. At around two-thirty, Adrian comes through the door. I stand wearily to greet him. There's love in his eyes as he gazes at Shay, and he speaks with genuine gratitude.

"You kept your word. I appreciate that, Havoc. How is she?"

"She held up through the worst of it. I'm just waiting to see her wake up."

"Do you mind if I wait here with you for a while?"

It seems odd for him to ask my permission. The last time he was this close to me, his hands were almost on my throat.

"Of course not. She's your daughter, Adrian."

We sit there waiting in silence, focused on Shay's vital signs, watching for any significant change, wishing for her eyes to flicker open, her mouth to move, her fingers to twitch, anything.

Eventually, Adrian says, "I'm proud of her, you know. She made a good life for herself. She's a better person than I could ever be."

"Maybe you should consider telling her that sometime, then."

"She doesn't want my love. In her eyes, I'm just a crook," Adrian says, shaking his head slowly.

I ponder whether it's wise to bring up the past with Adrian. After all that's happened in the last week, the last thing I need is a new enemy. I did, however, just risk my life to protect Shay's. Maybe another risk, this one for the possibility of more healing in her future, is worth a shot.

Oh, what the hell. "It isn't my business to fix things between the two of you. But if you really want to show her you care, you should try apologizing for what happened between you and her mother. She lost her brother and almost lost her life. I think it's way past time for you to explain why. Who knows how long any of us will survive in this city, anyway? Just say you're sorry and get it over with."

"You have a point, Havoc," Adrian acknowledges. If he's fazed by my bluntness, he doesn't show it.

"She's your daughter," I repeat. "I don't condone what you do, Adrian, but I can see you do seem to care about her. Motor City has made us all into what we are. You want to be a better father? Then choose to be."

He looks at me consideringly, then says, "Thanks, Harvey, for having her back."

"I didn't do it for you, Adrian. Shay's my partner; I did all of this for her."

He nods, and we lapse back into silence. Around three thirty, Adrian leaves to attend to his business. He tells me to let him know when Shay wakes up and gives me a number to contact him at. I struggle, but manage to enter it into my transponder with my left hand.

Around four, Walt stops by and brings me a sandwich. I eagerly chew as we talk. It finally puts an end to the persistent growling of my empty stomach and takes the edge off of my headache. He fills me in on some of the various casework from the Homicide Department, where he's taken charge of things, since Shay and I will be indisposed for the foreseeable future. After that, we bullshit for about a half hour, then Walt heads home. All is quiet again until five, when Carson shows up. He looks tired, but less stressed than yesterday.

"How are you two holding up?" he asks, sitting down beside me. There's a fresh cup of coffee in his hand, his vape clenched between his lips.

"Hanging in there."

"That's fortunate," Carson says, letting out a puff of vapor and sipping his coffee.

"How's the battle with the paperwork?"

"I just put the finishing touches on it. Mitchell and I made a public announcement about an hour ago. We filled everyone in on what we know so far."

"So it's done, then?" I don't feel as much of a sense of closure as I'd like. "I wish we knew why Anderson killed Chase and Martinez."

"I think the bastard took that to his grave. No way to know unless he said something to Shay." Carson nods in her direction.

"True."

"No offense, Harvey, but you look like shit. When was the last time you had a cup of coffee?" He raises his cup as he speaks.

"I don't remember, honestly."

"I can go get you one," Carson offers.

"No, that's OK, Carson. I'll get it myself. I could use a walk and some time to think."

"Suit yourself. I'll wait with her till you get back." He settles in dutifully.

At the far end of the hall, the bright LED screen of the in-wall Super K coffee kiosk dances with colorful options. I order up a large coffee with cream and sugar. As the kiosk prepares my drink, I close my eyes and think. *There has to be something I'm missing, some fact I've overlooked.*

My thoughts are interrupted by an alarm bell sounding from the kiosk. I open my eyes to see a message flashing across the screen. It states that there's no more cream available and asks if I would like a refund. I press the "Accept refund" bubble on the screen and take my free coffee. As I take my first sip of the bitter drink, an image floods into my mind. *Shit, Carson was drinking black coffee!* The cup slips from my hand. I don't see it spill onto the floor as I run down the hall toward Shay's room.

Bursting through the door, I see Carson near her bed. He slips whatever he's holding behind his back before I can identify it. A large bubble of air is passing through the narrow IV tube toward Shay's arm.

"Something wrong, Harvey?" Carson says, moving slightly away from her bedside.

"What the hell were you doing, Carson?"

A slow smile slides across his face. He takes his hand from behind his back, revealing an empty syringe. *I'm too late.*

"What the did you give her?"

"Nothing. Well, not exactly nothing," Carson says.

He sets the empty syringe on the table next to Shay's bed, then pulls a revolver from his jacket. It's my old gun, the one that backfired on Harris months ago. Carson must've taken it from the evidence room. He aims it at me, grinning. "I was hoping you would take a little more time getting your coffee. It would've been easier that way. I was planning for a quiet end to your partner. An air embolism, if you're wondering. Enough air introduced into the bloodstream near the brain will cause a stroke. Simple, yet hard to detect."

"You've lost it if you think you can get away with this," I growl.

"I like to think of myself as a survivor, Havoc. That's why I took the time to remove your gun from the evidence lockup. I fixed it up in case I needed it. And yes, the fingerprint ID is disabled. Tell me, why did you decide to come back so soon?"

"Black coffee at Jasper's apartment when he drinks it with cream. Black coffee in your hand just now. I'm betting the coffee in Anderson's office was you too, that you it planted to make me suspicious."

My reply makes Carson's grin widen, and he starts to laugh. "My God, Harvey, you have to be fucking kidding me. You figured it out because of *that*? I had black coffee at Jasper's because I knew the chief drank it that way. The coffee on Anderson's desk was his. You're telling me your light bulb moment is because the fucking coffee kiosk didn't have cream in it? I drink my coffee with cream and sugar!"

He shakes his head, never losing that maliciously prideful smile.

"Why kill Chase and Martinez?" I have nothing to lose by asking.

"Same reason I sent you on that drug bust. I always knew you were smart enough to be dangerous, Havoc. I was worried you might have heard too much from Johnathan. I figured Harris and Metzler would be able to get you out of my hair." He shakes his head ruefully. "It's hard to run drugs in this town when I have an officer as keen as you on the force. When those idiots failed, I thought I could be rid of you by recommending you for Homicide Division."

I lean warily back against the doorframe as he talks. I want to jump him and yank the IV from Shay's arm. The vital signs screen shows that her pulse is slowing. I'm powerless to stop her death, even though I've fought so hard to prevent it. All I can do now, before our end, is listen to Carson's smug confession as he monologues like a movie villain.

"Putting the chief in my pocket was as easy as drugging Johnathan and getting him to kill his wife," he continues. "I knew Anderson liked to see that call girl now and again. You know how people are when they take Tech; they get so hyperfocused on something that one idea planted at the right time can make them do almost anything. They don't always remember the real reason they did it, so they often create one instead. I slipped the chief a tablet of Tech in his coffee Sunday night before he left the office. Told him to kill May. Gave him the time and the place. He followed my orders to the letter. When he was done, I used Jasper's little surveillance tricks to make the evidence disappear. Of course, I still have the footage of Anderson fleeing the scene."

"But why Chase and Martinez?"

"It was unfortunate that they walked in on me when I was planting evidence on your pal Janet Carter. After that, I had no choice but to take care of them. I called in a bogus drug drop and waited there to take them out. I was going to plant the gun on Janet, and I went back to the crime scene to retrieve it from the storm drain I threw it down. Your partner caught me with it and sealed her fate by being too nosey. I had to call in a favor from Clay Kingston. That footage he fabricated for me ended up being just the ticket to send you on a rampage for Janet's blood. But you went and fucked that up for me by making amends with her before I got there."

"You did all of this for money?" I say, disgusted by his vile methods.

"Sure." He shrugs. "Money, power, all of it. This fucking town will suck the life out of you if you let it. I choose to be on top instead of on the bottom. Crime always pays better than law and order, Havoc. And who knows what will happen when the dust settles? I may even be the new chief!"

"We're on camera, Carson. Think again." I point at the camera on the wall.

"Wishful thinking, Havoc," he sneers. "Jasper's hacker tricks have served me well. As far as that camera's concerned, I'm not even here."

"What are you going to do?"

"A little more hacking magic will help me. When I'm done, it'll look like you shot yourself in despair on seeing your partner pass away. Footage from my office will put me there when it happens."

He seems to have thought of everything. I fight off despair and say, "You can't play this game forever, Carson. Someone will figure it out."

He snorts. "I already took down the chief of police and more than a dozen cops, not to mention your partner and now you. I don't think I'm going to lose much sleep over it, Havoc. "

As he says this, he starts to move toward me, raising the gun. On the screen beside Shay's bed, her vital signs spike. I see her hand twitch and her eyes flicker. *She's probably having a stroke, I think dismally. This is the end for us both.* I wish I could take back all of my mistakes. I wish I could've seen through Carson back when I had a chance to stop him. At least I get to go out with someone I respect. At least I'm with my partner at the end.

It takes a few agonizing seconds for me to realize what's happening. Behind Carson, Shay has risen from her bed. She takes a second to observe her surroundings, then grabs the closest weapon she can find, the syringe from the bedside table. With one smooth movement, she leaps forward and plunges the syringe into the side of Carson's neck, yanking out her IV as she latches her arms and legs around his torso like a cat clawing its way up a tree.

He stumbles, and his finger jerks on the trigger. I duck too slowly. The high-caliber bullet grazes my shoulder, tearing out a huge chunk of flesh. Shay pulls out the syringe and then stabs it into Carson's neck again and again. I jump on him and wrestle for the gun with my left hand. As I pull it from his fingers, another shot rings out.

As Carson's last breath escapes his body, he falls backward onto Shay, a gaping hole in his gut. Had the gun been aimed upward, the bullet would've gone through his back and into her. I struggle one-handed to pull his considerable weight off of her as she tries to push him away. We fight against his girth for a minute, then manage to get his corpse off of her. I use my good hand to help her to her feet. This sends pain through my fresh shoulder wound, on the opposite side from my broken wrist.

"I was trying to say it *wasn't* Anderson, it was Carson," Shay mumbles.

Fresh blood is spreading across her bandages, and she's spattered and dripping with Carson's blood, which is covering me too. The once-white room is a horror show in red, with a pool spreading from beneath Carson. If I wasn't so distracted by pain, I might be nauseated by the sight.

"Yeah. I … I just realized that a few minutes ago," I stammer.

"You're kind of a shitty detective, Havoc. Fortunately, you make up for it by being a great partner."

After this proclamation, Shay almost falls, adrenalin replaced by exhaustion. We're both struggling to stand on the now-slick floor. I reach my arm out to steady her, ignoring the pain. "I think you should get back in bed."

"Actually, in my leap of blind rage, my catheter came out in addition to my IV. I really need to take a piss," she says, almost laughing.

I chuckle and put her arm around my good shoulder to help her out of the room. We must appear deranged, bloodied and broken as we are. *Motor City put us through the damn wood chipper, and somehow, we came out the other side intact—well, mostly, anyway.* I support Shay's weight as best I can. With her free hand, she puts pressure on the bandages that cover her chest. As officers come rushing down the hall, we go right past them toward the bathroom. I am intent on helping Shay make this last effort before both of us collapse.

Mitchell is among the gathering crowd. "Havoc! Smith!" she calls out. "What the bloody hell is going on here? Talk to me."

Shay does. "I have to pee!"

She lets go of me and shakily transfers her weight to the doorframe as she goes into the bathroom. Mitchell looks to me for an explanation. I prop myself up against the wall before I reply, unable to stand on my own any longer.

"Carson's dead, ma'am."

"What?" Mitchell asks, eyes wide with disbelief.

"He was the brains behind the drug operation that almost got me killed. After that, he dosed the chief with Tech to convince him to murder May. He killed Jasper to keep it quiet, and Chase and Martinez because they saw him tamper with evidence. The bastard was in on it with Metzler and Harris. This whole shitstorm started with Johnathan getting cold feet. Carson set everything else off to cover up his drug operation. Shay realized that Chase and Martinez's deaths were connected to the others. When she went back to the crime scene yesterday morning, she ran into Carson there." All this explaining is making me tired.

"I sincerely hope you can back all of this up with proof, Havoc," Mitchell says.

I nod. "Yes, ma'am. He just tried to kill Detective Smith and myself. If you look into his smart desk, you'll find the software he used to mess with the security footage. One of the hackers we looked into helped Carson fake evidence against Janet Carter. A talk with him will set the rest straight."

The toilet flushes, and Shay stumbles out of the bathroom. I abandon the security of the wall so I can help support her.

"Havoc tells me that Sergeant Carson is the one who shot you yesterday. Is that true?" Mitchell asks Shay.

"Yes, ma'am. It was all Carson. Except for May. Anderson killed her," Shay replies, still holding her chest.

Dr. Arnold is hurrying toward us. I glance across the hall and see the twin trails of blood Shay and I have left behind us, mine from my shoulder, Shay's from her chest wounds. With that and the blood from Carson's fatal injury, the hall looks like a scene from a slaughterhouse.

Mitchell leaves us in Dr. Arnold's care. Nurses arrive and help us walk to the elevator, and we ride with them and the doctor up one floor. They take us to a room with two beds and two monitoring screens. One of the nurses changes Shay's bandages and helps her into a clean hospital gown while the other helps Arnold tend to my shoulder. They put us each on a fresh IV and give us something for the pain. By the time they're finished, Shay has fallen back asleep. The clock on my monitor reads just after seven. I ask Dr. Arnold a question that has been on my mind since Shay woke up.

"Hey, doc, how come Shay survived the air embolism?"

"Most people don't know the truth behind trying to induce such an embolism," he explains. "It would take at least a few syringes full of air to work. And you'd have to keep the air bubble large enough to interrupt the blood flow to the brain, because there are two separate filters that would break it up before it could reach her veins. Still, she's lucky you came in before he had the chance to finish the job."

After checking Shay once more, Dr. Arnold leaves the room. I watch as Shay's chest rises and falls gently, her electric blue hair a stark contrast to the white of the bedsheets. *How the hell did she survive this? How did I survive it?* I think about letting Rina know I'm OK, but the idea fades and I fall into a deep sleep.

I wake up Tuesday morning feeling as close to normal as I can considering my wounds. I get up and enjoy the convenience of the en-suite bathroom. I throw some water on my face and wipe it off with a towel. The swelling has gone down, and the bruises are starting to fade around the edges. I leave the restroom and find that in my brief absence, Shay has awoken.

"We get our own toilet? This room is awesome," Shay says.

I smile and go over to her bedside. She sits up a little to bring our conversation to eye level.

"How do you feel?" I ask.

"Probably better than I look," Shay says. "And I could kill for a cigarette."

My smile widens. The blue in her eyes shimmers. This might be the calmest I've seen them.

"I think I look way worse than I feel; don't think I can help with the cigarette either," I say ruefully.

"Yeah, I guess that wouldn't go over too well in here. Who beat you up so bad? Was that Anderson?" Shay asks, one eyebrow raised.

"Yeah, old bastard really put up a fight. I owe him thanks for this too." I raise my right arm in the sling.

"Damn. Broke my wrist once. That one sucked," Shay says, wincing in sympathy.

"Yeah." We contemplate my wrist solemnly. Then my curiosity gets the better of me. "So, what happened when you went back to the crime scene Sunday morning?"

"When I woke up, it occurred to me that there was something off. The blood patterns and lack of signs of a struggle suggested that the officers knew their killer. I was just going to drive by and look around real quick, then wait in my car until you got there. Carson was there when I arrived, though. It didn't seem that strange to me at first. Chase and Martinez were officers under his command. Wouldn't be that weird for him to be there."

"What tipped you off?"

"Nothing, exactly. He seemed nervous, I guess. He was sharp and rude. Acted like he didn't want me to be there, like he was hiding something. Before I realized what was happening, he pulled his gun on me."

I nod. "He told me he'd gone back to get the gun so he could plant it on Janet. Had he gotten the chance, he would've been able to place the blame on Janet for Chase and Martinez as well as you. All with that same gun and some fabricated footage he had Clay Kingston make for him."

"I knew I didn't like that Clay sleazebag. I look forward to wiping the smirk off his face," Shay says, pressing her lips together tightly.

"This whole story is so crazy, I wouldn't believe it if it hadn't happened to us."

With no warning, Shay bridges the gap between us. She plants her lips on my cheek. The peppermint lip balm on them stings the scratch from my fight with Anderson. She moves her head back and looks deep into my eyes.

"Thanks, Harvey. You saved my ass."

I shrug, flustered. "It's my job."

She shakes her head, then gently punches me in the shoulder. I wince in pain.

"Shit, I forgot," Shay says, cringing.

"It's OK. Thanks for saving my ass too."

I send Rina a message letting her know I'm all right, then Shay and I have some breakfast. Later in the day, Walt and Rina return, and Shay and I retell our story as they hang on every word. It seems so incredible that we lived through this, that we survived everything Motor City threw at us. We brought down two high-ranking dirty cops and a handful of their underlings, and we even solved four murders, all in one week. Shay and I may be here recovering for a while, but I'm glad to have the chance to rest.

CHAPTER 16

UNEXPECTED END

Motor City has proved once again how tough she really is. Despite the initial uproar, the public is relieved to know that there are two fewer corrupt leaders in the department. The media spins Shay and me as heroes of the highest caliber. For now, we're celebrities. I'm glad that the city has taken the higher road, relieved it chose to see past its flaws and cherish its successes. The truth has saved its dark streets so that they might have the chance to grow brighter.

I pull the hearse up to the curb outside Shay's apartment and let it idle as I wait. Outside the windshield, the wind blows dust around the street. It's late fall now. Soon it will be winter, a season that brings a whole other dimension to the vast streets of our asphalt jungle.

Shay and I have technically been on medical leave until this morning. Our injuries didn't keep us from seeing each other over the last few months of our recovery, though. Strangely enough, I have her nasty smoking habit to thank for our keeping in touch.

I ended up bringing her coffee every few days as an excuse to check her apartment for cigarettes. It's amazing, all the clever places she tries to hide them. At first, my efforts pissed her off, but I think she actually appreciates them now. Arnold gave her an advanced patch system to help curb the nicotine cravings. I've been his second line of defense, armed with caffeine and bags of suckers instead of prescriptions. A few times, I even managed to convince Shay to come over and have dinner with Rina and me instead of holing up in her apartment and chewing through endless Dum Dums.

A few weeks after the action that almost got us both killed, we were given the chance to go with Walt to take down Clay Kingston. Walt tracked him to a suburb outside of Motor City. Though we were only allowed to observe the operation, Shay and I enjoyed seeing the little weasel get what he deserved. It's refreshing to know that everyone involved in Carson's far-ranging scheme is off of Motor City's streets. *How fitting that a case that began with a hacker should end with one.*

After a few minutes, Shay emerges from the apartment. If she would've taken any longer, I would've been inclined to go check behind the sink for another hidden pack of cigarettes. She opens the door and slides in. The wound on her neck is healed, its jagged scar a permanent reminder of her brush with death. When I apologized for having made it worse than just a bullet wound, she laughed and told me she liked it.

"Did our friend Sue bring the Eldorado over yesterday?" Shay asks once she's seated beside me.

"Yep, dropped it off around three."

Unfortunately, in the time that Shay's car was parked at the crime scene, someone broke the driver's-side window and busted the ignition in a failed attempt to steal it. Feeling somewhat responsible and slightly guilty, I ordered a piece of glass for it from a salvage yard out west. I later found an ignition switch in a nearby parts warehouse.

"Think we'll have time to work on it after work tonight?" Shay asks hopefully.

"It'll probably have to be a Saturday ordeal."

"Damn. I suppose that means I have to ride with you all week, then. You and your sister may even force me to eat stir fry on Saturday," Shay says with a smirk.

I smile back. "I think you might be right."

We drive off toward the department, winding easily through the streets. I back into my spot in the garage, and we walk into the station. Walt covered for us during our absence and kept me well informed. Shay and I take our place at the head of the room. Unlike on my first day as lead, all forty-nine pairs of eyes remain trained on me.

"Walt has been keeping me updated on your cases. I'm glad to know that you're out there keeping the city safe," I say. "The most important thing I've learned in the last month is that anything can happen in this city. We don't always know who we can trust, so watch your back. Expect the unexpected. Take care of yourselves, and watch out for your partners. If you can do that, you can survive Motor City. You might even make it a better place in the process."

To my surprise, the other detectives give me a brief round of applause. As they disperse, Walt comes up to speak with Shay and me. "Got a double homicide for you on the far end of town. I sent you the info. Oh, and Mitchell wants to talk to you, Harvey."

I toss the keys to Shay. She snatches them out of the air. "Meet up with you at the car in a minute, then?" Shay asks.

"Sure. I'll bring us some coffee on my way back."

I head up to see Mitchell. I realize, as I enter the elevator, that the last time I was upstairs, Anderson was chief. In the wake of his and Carson's transgressions, Mitchell became the new chief of police. The automated assistant indifferently greets me as I come into the hall. I notice straight off when I enter the office that Mitchell has changed the decor. Instead of having lavish and over-the-top furnishings, the office is clean and neat, populated by tasteful chairs and desks with a modern theme. I take a seat in a nice chair across from Mitchell's smart desk.

"Good to see that you're doing well, Havoc," she says. "It's an honor to have you and your partner back."

"Thank you, ma'am. It's good to be back."

"I have a few things to discuss with you. First, I wonder if you would answer a personal question?"

"Sure."

"Why did you and your partner decide to stay with the department? Both of you are more than qualified for retirement," Mitchell says, leaning back in her chair.

I chew on her question. The thought of a simple retired life was tantalizing. In the first few weeks after Carson and Anderson's demise, I was planning to retire. I could have become a mechanic; I might have enjoyed being a private investigator as well. Eventually, I decided that I would miss the excitement, and more than that, I would miss working with Shay. We only had a week together on the job, and it was horrible in a lot of ways. But I felt more alive in that one week with her than I had in my whole life. Staying on will be worth it for her alone. But my innermost thoughts are too personal to share with Mitchell, so I decide to simplify things.

"I can't speak to my partner's reasons. I chose to stay because it's what I do, and I'm good at it."

Mitchell nods. "Very well. I would like to extend my gratitude to you, Havoc. I have yet to fill my old position in the department, or Carson's. Would you be interested in either one?"

"I appreciate the offer, ma'am. I think I would prefer to remain lead detective, though."

"Fair enough. Do you have any recommendations for either position?" Mitchell asks, curiosity in her eyes.

I bite my lip in thought. Ideas flicker on like light bulbs. "I think Walt would be an excellent choice for Carson's position. And you know Anteka Sokola, I'm sure."

"Yes. I'm rather impressed by her work in the Narcotics lab."

"Well, I think Anteka would be a fine choice to fill your old position."

Mitchell thinks this over, then says, "Agreed. Thank you for your recommendations. I would also like to thank you for your exemplary service. Be sure to thank your partner for me as well."

"I will. And thank you, chief."

A small smile turns up the corners of her lips. Mitchell is the right leader for this department. She deserves the success.

I go back downstairs, getting Shay and me each a cup of coffee from one of the in-wall Super K kiosks along the way. As I carry our beverages out to the car, I realize that everything in this case ultimately hinged on the kiosk being out of cream. I may not have made the connection about Carson in time if it hadn't been for that one fluke. Was it luck or fate? Maybe a bit of both.

I find Shay in the hearse, the engine idling. I slide into the old Cadillac and pass her a coffee.

"What did Mitchell want?" she asks.

"She wanted me to thank you for your efforts."

"And?"

"And to offer me her old job or Carson's."

"And?" Shay repeats.

"I told her I like my position."

"How come I didn't get that offer?" She frowns.

"I don't know. She did ask me if I had anyone in mind for the empty positions, though."

"Shit, you better not have spoken for me, Harvey. I like being a detective," Shay says, narrowing her eyes in disapproval.

"Actually, I told her to give Carson's job to Walt and her old job to Tek."

Shay almost spits out her coffee. "Holy shit! That'll really surprise them! Awesome!"

"I thought so too."

We sit there and sip our coffee. The engine of the old hearse lopes expectantly, as if she's as excited for another case as we are. Motor City waits outside the parking garage for the three of us. *This is it; this is the life. I finally feel like I am where I should be. Detective Harvey Havoc.* I savor the moment.

Shay disrupts my pleasant musings. "You stuck there, partner?"

"Sorry, I was just thinking."

"What about?" she asks.

"I'm glad to be here. Glad you're my partner."

"Don't get all mushy on me now, Harvey. I might slip and say I'm glad you're my partner too. Can't have that."

Her sarcasm makes us both smile.

"What have we got on this double homicide so far?" I say, getting down to business.

"Not much. Don't think we're going to have a good picture of it until we see it in person. Report says the crime scene's a mess."

"Well, we certainly know how to deal with messes."

Shay shakes her head and laughs a little. "True."

I smile and look into her vibrant eyes. "All right, let's go kick some ass."

Shay grins, grabbing ahold of the armrest on the door to brace herself. Just for the hell of it, I flip on the lights and siren. Elli's tires squeal in protest as we fly out of the garage and onto the streets of Motor City. Shay turns up the rock station loud enough to hear above the high-pitched wail of the siren.

Motor City may be dark, it may be deadly, and it will likely succeed in killing us one day. Not in this moment, though. In this moment, Motor City is ours. Shay and I are its first line of defense: now, *we* control the havoc.

THE HAVOC WILL CONTINUE WITH

THE TECHNICIAN'S GAME

247

THE HAVOC WILL CONTINUE WITH

THE TECHNICIAN'S GAME